... must like the

...! MASSIVE thanks also to (drum roll, please):

CORDELIA AND TASLIMA – my best buds EVER – always there to make me laugh and believe I can do this!

MUM AND DAD – sometimes you're so embarrassing. I'll try and stay out of trouble. No promises, though. ☺

PIP – my lipstick-loving little sis – don't grow up too fast!!

MAGNUS (THE MAGNIFICENT) – you gave me a bite of your muffin. Remember, in biology?

Some things you NEVER forget!

Finally, I'm dedicating this to the dolphins, butterflies and all the endangered creatures on our planet. I'm GOING to make a difference (Twig – I told you I would!).

I'm going to be your star!

**Love,
Sassy Wilde xxx**

Seriously Sassy

Maggi Gibson

JF

PUFFIN

In memory of Maggie Evans
who helped Sassy take her first steps

PUFFIN BOOKS

Published by the Penguin Group
Penguin Books Ltd, 80 Strand, London WC2R ORL, England
Penguin Group (USA) Inc., 375 Hudson Street, New York, New York 10014, USA
Penguin Group (Canada), 90 Eglinton Avenue East, Suite 700, Toronto, Ontario, Canada M4P 2Y3
(a division of Pearson Penguin Canada Inc.)
Penguin Ireland, 25 St Stephen's Green, Dublin 2, Ireland (a division of Penguin Books Ltd)
Penguin Group (Australia), 250 Camberwell Road, Camberwell, Victoria 3124, Australia
(a division of Pearson Australia Group Pty Ltd)
Penguin Books India Pvt Ltd, 11 Community Centre, Panchsheel Park, New Delhi – 110 017, India
Penguin Group (NZ), 67 Apollo Drive, Rosedale, North Shore 0632, New Zealand
(a division of Pearson New Zealand Ltd)
Penguin Books (South Africa) (Pty) Ltd, 24 Sturdee Avenue, Rosebank, Johannesburg 2196, South Africa

Penguin Books Ltd, Registered Offices: 80 Strand, London WC2R ORL, England

puffinbooks.com

First published 2009
1

Text copyright © Maggi Gibson, 2009
Illustrations copyright © Hennie Haworth, 2009
All rights reserved

The moral right of the author and illustrator has been asserted

Set in 13/16 pt Monotype Baskerville by
Palimpsest Book Production Limited, Grangemouth, Stirlingshire
Made and printed in England by Clays Ltd, St Ives plc

British Library Cataloguing in Publication Data
A CIP catalogue record for this book is available from the British Library

ISBN: 978-0-141-32464-7

www.greenpenguin.co.uk

TRACK ONE

Oh why can't people be more like dolphins?
A dolphin's face always meets you grinning
A dolphin is free – he's got no need to kill
A dolphin is happy – he swims for the thrill.

A dolphin just wants to live in the ocean
He doesn't pollute, he ain't got no notion
Of nuclear bombs and nuclear fusion
Or killing, or wars, or starting aggression.

Oh why can't people be more like dolphins?
A dolphin's face always meets you grinning
He don't need no factories pumping out smoke
He don't need no bombs, he doesn't kill folk.

He don't build no roads, he don't poison the air
And we're killing his world, acting like we don't care
It makes me so sad, it makes me so mad
The planet's in crisis, it's us are to blame.

Oh why can't people be more like dolphins?
I don't wanna be human, I can't stand the shame
But what can I do, 'cept stand up and sing
Don't ruin our world. No! Not in my name!

By Sassy Wilde

I

'So what do you think?' I ask as I prop my guitar back on its stand.

Cordelia and Taslima are round for a girls' night in and I've just sung them my latest song. Mr Hemphead, that's our biology teacher, was telling us yesterday about how the oceans are warming up, and how humans are to blame with all their cars and factories and everything, but it's the fish and sea creatures that are suffering. I felt so angry I wrote the song earlier today.

Cordelia's a Dolly Goth. Her hair's as black as a bat's eyeball, and she wears it tied high in bunches with big scarlet ribbons.

'It's great, Sass.' She grins, looking up from painting tiny white skulls on her black fingernails. 'All your songs are, but I've got a hunch that *this* is the one, you know, to make you a star!'

I can't help but smile. Cordelia's psychic, on account of her mum being a witch, and more often than not her hunches are right. Even when it's crazy things, like what's the square root of 34,563 or the date of the Battle of Inverknockynooky.[1]

'Yeah, I loved it too.' Taslima smiles, picking up my guitar. 'But what I *really* want to know (strum strum strum) is what's going on between you (strum strum strum) and the gorgeous (STRUM STRUM STRUM) Magnus Menzies?'

'Nothing!' I protest, trying not to blush. 'He offered me a bite of his muffin in biology. That's all.'

I pick up Tiny Ted and fire him at the mini-basketball hoop on the back of the door. His arm gets caught on the ring and he dangles dangerously. Which is pretty much how I've been feeling ever since I bit into Magnus's muffin.

'But it was chocolate chip and you never ever eat chocolate!' Cordelia protests. 'And you've been all starry-eyed ever since. So give, Sassy! What's going on?'

'I don't know,' I sigh. 'I mean it was only a bite of a muffin –' Tiny Ted loses his grip and plummets to the floor.

'Only a bite of a muffin!' Taslima's eyebrows

[1] 1312.

shoot up under her fringe. 'Sassy! When a boy offers a girl a bite of his muffin, well, it's like he's saying, I really, really fancy you.' Taslima wants to be a psychologist when she grows up. She insists on reading meaning into the tiniest, most innocent of actions.

'Yeah, sure, little Miss Freud,' I laugh. 'But right now boys are NOT part of my life plan. I don't have time for them. I've got more than enough to do as it is, thank you.'

'Yeah, like the planet to save,' Cordelia says dreamily as she flicks through a mag she's just pulled out of her Scary Cat bag.

'And my career to get off the ground,' I add, taking the guitar from Taslima. 'I've not even got my first demo disc yet!'

'So let me get this right, Sass,' Taslima says, her brow furrowed in a professional-psychologist sort of way. 'It's not enough to just *write* a brilliant song?'

'Course not!' I protest. 'I mean, if you write a song, it's cos you want people to hear it, you want to be up there in front of the lights, belting it out, don't you?'

I start tuning the guitar. 'It's so depressing (twang) I'm thirteen already (twang) next thing (twang) I'll be thirty (twang) then I'll be dead.'

'So can we get back to the subject?' Cordelia

5

fixes me with a green-eyed lie-to-me-and-I'll-turn-you-into-a-toad stare.[2] 'You have no feelings at all for Magnus?'

'Oh, I don't know . . .' I mutter.

Cordelia's eyes widen dangerously.

'OK! OK!' I give in. 'I do feel all squidgy when I see him . . . and I've only ever felt like that before about tiny panda cubs, or fluffy little baby seals, but –'

'So face up to it!' Taslima exclaims. 'Look, Sass, you don't really have a choice. It's your hormones. You know when you leaned in to take a bite of his muffin? You must have got a whiff of his pheromones –'

'Fairy gnomes?' I interrupt.

'P-H-E-R-O-M-O-N-E-S,' Taslima spells it out. 'Like an invisible smell people put out to attract a mate.'

'Aren't all smells invisible?' I ask, confused.

'The thing is,' Taslima continues excitedly, 'his boy pheromones probably met up with your girl pheromones and they fizzled together like a chemical cocktail, so now you don't have a choice. It's hormonal. A teen thing. You're destined to go all squidgy every time you see him –'

[2] Did I mention her mum is training her in the Dark Arts? When she's eighteen she'll be a fully fledged witch with her own private broomstick. Scary!

'Never mind hormones!' Cordelia squeals, flapping her mag. 'This is Mum's *Wiccan Weekly*. You're Scorpio, Sass, that right?'

I nod.

'Well, here's what Psychic Psandra says: *Red alert, Scorpio! The guy of your dreams is hovering nearby. Keep your broomstick polished to a sheen. Soon you and he will be heading for the stars.*'

'Cordelia!' I laugh, chucking a cushion at her. 'You can't take that junk seriously!'

'But you must!' Cordelia exclaims, her green eyes shining. 'Don't you see? You and Magnus? It's kismet. Destiny! Why fight it?'

Once Cordelia and Taslima have gone, I shower and change into my Greenpeace nightie. Then I close the bedroom curtains and switch on my Planet Earth lamp. It casts a beautiful blue light across the room. My crystal mobile tinkles gently in the breeze from the open window. The big polar bear on my wall poster gazes down from his white wonderland. I pick up my guitar and start to gently strum.

I really do need to cut a demo disc soon, but who knows when I'll ever have enough money. Earlier today I counted my savings. It didn't take long. Last year I adopted a donkey in the Dorset Donkey Sanctuary and that takes up most of my poverty-level pocket money.

Softly I start to sing my dolphin song again. It

makes me so angry to think about the oceans being poisoned, the ice caps melting, the forests disappearing . . .

And it's up to me and my generation to put things right. I don't care about hormones or kismet or anything else. I know what I want to do with my life, what's really important to me, and I really don't have time for all this silly Magnus stuff.

2

It's Monday morning now. The weekend has whizzed by and I've hardly anything to show for it. Just my dolphin song and one complaints letter to the Chief Executive of Paradiso's, our local supermarket.

33 Anton Drive
Strathcarron

The Chief Executive
Paradiso's Supermarkets
Milton Keynes

Dear Sir,

I would be grateful if you would stop supplying free plastic carrier bags to your customers. Immediately. And remove all other plastic packaging from your foodstuffs.
   Plastic is the curse of the planet. It is NOT biodegradable. Did you know that 1lb of plastic

*breaks up into 100,000 tiny pieces in the ocean,
making it look like plankton? Fish and dolphins and
whales then swallow it, mistaking it for food.*

*It may surprise you, but there's now six times
MORE plastic than plankton in the North Pacific.
And it's toxic. So the whole food chain is being
poisoned.*

*How would you like to have a plateful of plastic
for your dinner then wake up with a terminal tummy
ache?*

*Yours faithfully,
Sassy Wilde*

*PS Your advertising slogan — 'Paradiso's, the
supermarket that makes shopping heavenly' — is simply
not true. My mother drags me to Paradiso's once a
week. And it's hell!*

On the way downstairs for breakfast I check
in the bathroom mirror and, sure enough, right
in the centre of my forehead a big choccy-fuelled
spot is roaring up, red and angry. I so wish I'd
refused that bite of Magnus's muffin! I pull a few
curls down over it, but it's no use, they just bounce
back up again.

In the kitchen Mum is slumped at the table,
half asleep, reading her latest self-help book, *How
to Raise a Well-balanced Teen*. I don't blame her for

swotting up. Pip – that's my little sis – is only nine, but already she's addicted to MTV. And she's planning a career as a glamour model. Right now she's perched on a bar stool flicking through one of her Lolitaz magazines. Lolitaz, the latest craze among tweenies, are twenty-centimetre-high dolls, with the most grotesque faces, all goldfish lips and pussy-cat eyes with huge fluttery lashes. When Pip turns teen she's going to be such a nightmare. Then my parentals will appreciate just how easy *I* am.

Dad pops some toast, spreads it with honey and tosses it in front of Mum. Dad's a morning person. It suits him to be bristling about the place, brewing tea, scattering coffee grains everywhere.

I'm just making myself a delicious wake-up smoothie, chopping some banana and kiwi and wondering how many food miles the fruits have travelled and how much that's contributed to global warming, and whether or not I should feel guilty, when Dad whips off his frilly apron and clears his throat.

'I've something important to tell you. Something that could affect all our futures,' he says, then glances at the clock. 'So we'll have a Family Meet at four, OK?'

'But, Dad, you don't even finish work till six,' I protest.

'Not tonight,' he says, grabbing his briefcase.

'I want us all here at four. Now this is important. There's someone I want you to meet.'

And he's gone! Which is pretty typical of his odd behaviour this past couple of weeks. Always disappearing, staying out late, having whispered phone conversations.

'What's Dad on about?' I ask Mum.

'Nothing to do with me,' she yawns, without looking up, even though I know her book says, *Always give your teen a proper answer; shrugging them off could cause untold psychological damage.*

Just then Pip gives a little squeal, leaps from her stool and boogies across the kitchen in her lacy black negligee and pink kitten-heeled mules. Honestly! I can't believe the way Mum lets Pip dress sometimes. And, what's more, Pip's had earplugs in all along, so hasn't heard a word Dad said. She's off on Planet Pip.

Then the big grandfather clock in the hall booms. Nine o'clock. Which fortunately it isn't or I'd be late for school. Mum sets it half an hour fast, because that way, she says, we'll never be late. (Sometimes I doubt my mum's sanity.) I down my smoothie, pull on my jacket, grab my bag and give our old dog, Brewster, a quick tummy tickle, then dash out of the door.

It's lunchtime before I get the chance to REALLY chat to Taslima and Cordelia. There are ears everywhere in our school. (Usually on the side of teachers' heads.) So we link arms and head for our special place, round the back, up three stairs, in the doorway. We found this hidey-hole when we first started high school and Hannah Harrison from Third Year plus her sidekicks – including Megan Campbell who was once, in the mists of time, my bestest friend ever – were trying to terrorize us. But that's all in the past now.

'You do know this is a fire door,' Cordelia says as we snuggle down on the top step. 'Which means,' she continues, 'if there's a fire and all the people inside rush out, they'll be saved, but we'll be tragically trampled to death.'[3]

'Never mind dying,' I mutter. 'I've got a real problem.'

Taslima looks delighted. She just loves problems. She whips out a tiny pink notebook, licks her pencil and arches one eyebrow. It's psychologist's body language, apparently, for DO GO ON.

'My dad's been behaving strangely,' I begin.

Cordelia snorts and tosses her long hair. 'What's new? Your family are all totally weird.'

[3] Cordelia has this strange death fascination thing. I was a bit morbid myself when I was ten. I even wrote MY LAST WILL AND TESTAMENT and left instructions for my funeral. It was to be a happy and joyous celebration of my tragically short life. No flowers, please. All donations to Save the Dolphins.

A bit rich coming from Cordelia, the Dolly Goth! But I decide to rise above it.

'Anyway,' I continue, 'he's hardly been at home these past few weeks. And when he is, he heads straight for his study. I've heard him on the phone too. Late at night. To someone called Digby.'

'Digby?' Cordelia echoes. 'What kind of name is that?'

I shrug. Sometimes Cordelia asks questions which cannot be answered.

'Have you tried checking his email and text messages?' Taslima suggests.

I shake my head. 'He's locked them with a password. Something else he's never done before. And now he's called a Family Meet for four and he doesn't even finish work till six. He says it's important we're all there. It's something that could affect all our futures. *And* there's someone he wants us to meet.'

Taslima chews the end of her pencil. 'What's your mum saying?' she asks quietly.

'Not a lot. She just seems totally stressed. In fact, she's been acting weird for weeks. They both have. You know the way, they're in the kitchen or the living room or wherever, talking about something, and you walk in and there's this AWFUL silence.'

'Sounds like a serious relationship problem.' Taslima nods wisely. 'Now, if it had been a *woman* he'd been phoning –'

'I hope you don't mind me asking,' Cordelia cuts across Taslima. 'I mean this is just a hunch. A kinda gut feelingy thing.'

'Go on,' I say. 'Spill!'

'It's just an idea,' Cordelia begins slowly, 'but has your dad changed his appearance recently?'

I think about it for a moment. What self-respecting girl actually LOOKS at her dad? Dads are dads. They're just there. And then it strikes me. 'Yep! He's had his hair cut in this ridiculous way. Like he thinks he's cool. *And* he's started using hair gel.'

'I don't know how to put this, er, delicately.' Cordelia drops her voice to a whisper. 'But is it possible, just maybe, that your dad's gay?'

3

My imagination is often referred to as overactive. As in, *Sassy would do well in English if only she could rein in her overactive imagination.*

Usually I think my OI is a real asset. For example, it's my OI that stops me from dying of complete boredom in maths. I can copy perfectly well from Taslima, who sits next to me and whose brain is like a calculator, while my OI is up and off out of the window swimming with the dolphins, or getting up on stage to collect my first Brit Award.

But there's a downside to my OI. Someone just needs to plant the seed of an idea – like my dad might be gay – and, wey-hey, suddenly it's sprouted into a little plant. Then the eensy-weensy plant grows bigger, then bigger and bigger, till it's a huge great beanstalk, and I'm struggling among all the leaves and branches in a total panic.

But then again, I remind myself, Cordelia's

hunch might be wrong. I mean, maybe Dad's not gay. Maybe Digby is just a new friend or work colleague.

But if Digby is a work colleague why would he be calling him late at night? And why would Dad be out so much in the evenings?

I get myself into such a tizz in English that when Magnus turns round and smiles at me I totally blank him. Then I feel bad about it, cos I really didn't mean to be rude.

The thing is, the more I think about Cordelia's 'gay dad' theory the more sense it makes. I mean, Mum and Dad haven't exactly been playing perfect partners recently. There have been quite a few rows. Especially about Dad rushing home for tea then rushing back out again. Mum even threw her *Little Book of Calm* at him last week.

As the afternoon ticks towards three o'clock my imagination desperately tries to come up with other possibilities. I make a list down the margin of my history notebook:

1. Digby is Dad's love child from before he met Mum.
2. Dad was adopted, but never knew it, and Digby is his long-lost little brother.
3. Digby is a code name. Dad is a government spy and his cover's been blown and we're

being sent to live in Reykjavik or Beijing or somewhere.[4]

That's as far as I get before the bell rings for home time.

After school Taslima and Cordelia walk home with me. When we stop at the gate Brewster bumbles down the path to meet us.

'Over here, boy,' I call as he sticks his nose in the air, trying to sniff me out. Brewster's a spotless Dalmatian. At least, that's what Dad told me when I was three. (I was all of five before I realized there was no such thing.) Anyway, Brewster's fifteen, which means in doggy years he's one hundred and five. Oh, and he's blind.

Cordelia tickles Brewster's ears and he points his nose adoringly at her. 'Maybe best not have Brewster in the Family Meet,' she says. 'The shock might kill him.'

Then my two best mates in the whole wide world hug me and I force myself up the garden path towards the front door. Dad's car is in the drive, parked behind Mum's like it's stopping her from getting out. Pip will be home already, so they're probably all waiting.

I stop in the hall and peer through the glass

[4] Told you I had an overactive imagination, didn't I?

door into the kitchen. There's no sign of Pip or Mum. Dad's there, busily making coffee. And he's not alone. There's a young man with him. They're talking and laughing together, and I can't help noticing the young man's wearing a suit and a lilac shirt and a pink tie. And I know I shouldn't make assumptions about people because of what they wear, but I can't help thinking, *What if Cordelia's hunch is right? What if this is Dad's new boyfriend?!*

I take a deep breath and go in.

'Sassy, I'd like you to meet Digby,' Dad says. Then he puts an arm round the young man's shoulder and they both grin at me, like the happy couple!

'I've heard all about you, Sassy.' Digby smiles nervously. 'I'm sure we're going to get on just brilliantly.'

I pull back a chair and plonk myself huffily down on it. There's an assortment of cakes on a plate in the centre of the table: two cream doughnuts, two eclairs and a huge meringue. Meringue's my fave. My tummy betrays me and rumbles noisily. My mouth's no better. It starts watering.

Scowling, I fold my arms across my chest.

Finally Dad stops struggling with the cafetière and puts five mugs out on the worktop. Just then Pip bounces in. Her eyes alight on the cakes and she's ecstatic. She grins at Digby and hugs Dad. One cream doughnut and Pip has sold out!

But I can't be bought so easily. I'm holding back till I find out what Dad's up to. I mean, if he's about to tell us that Digby is his new partner or his long-lost love child, then he can stuff his meringue.

There's an awkward silence as we wait for Mum. It gets to the point where I really can't stand it any more.

'Dad, I'm not sure I want to hear what you're going to say,' I blurt. 'I'm perfectly happy with our family the way it is.'

'Delighted to hear it,' says Mum, who's just floated in looking absolutely stunning in a tight-fitting dress and sexy shoes. 'I'll remind you of that next time you're begging to be put up for adoption.'

Digby stares at her in a decidedly un-gay way and leaps forward to pull out a chair.

'Thank you, Digby.' She smiles. 'And now, Angus, maybe you'd like to tell the girls what you and Digby are up to.'

Dad puffs himself up to his full height.

'OK, girls.' He clears his throat dramatically. 'Your father is going into politics.'

I can hardly believe my ears. Did he just say *going into politics*? I mean, my father does not have a political follicle in his entire body! I can never get him to support any good causes. Only last month I tried to get him to take part in 'Give It Up for the Planet Day'. All he had to do was agree to sell our car and use a bike instead. But he totally refused.

'The point is,' Dad explains, 'the town hall is rife with corruption. Someone's got to do something. There's a general election coming up. And, to cut a long story short, I'm proud to report I've been accepted as a candidate.'

I stare at Dad, mouth open. I mean, why couldn't he just have said that at breakfast? And saved me hours of agony and mental torture? If I end up in therapy it's going to be all his fault. I hope MPs earn lots of money cos he's gonna have to pay for it.

'Young Digby here has offered to be my election agent,' Dad says. 'So he's going to be around the house a lot from now on, masterminding the campaign.'

Digby beams at us.

'Now obviously I've discussed this with your mother,' Dad continues, 'and she's on board. So now I'd like you two to tell me what you think.'

He says *you two* but he stares at me. As usual, as First Born and Older Sister, I have to shoulder ALL the responsibility. Next time I must make sure to be born second.

'Yeah, sure, cool,' I say as I reach for the

meringue before someone else bags it. 'I mean, what you do in your own time's your business.'[5]

'Ah, but not quite, Sassy,' Digby says. 'We need to be sure you're fully on-side.' He fixes me with a freaky stare.

'What Digby's saying is this –' Dad sits down opposite me – 'when the election campaign starts in a couple of days' time, the whole family will be in the spotlight. Unless you promise you'll behave, then there's no point in me standing.'

I'm about to protest that I always behave when Mum cuts in. 'To put it bluntly, Sassy, a repetition of the Paradiso's Panties Incident could ruin your father's chances.'

I sigh heavily. Whenever my parentals want to get at me they bring up the Paradiso's Panties Incident.

'Those knickers were being made in sweatshops by tiny kids working for slave wages!' I splutter, spraying flakes of meringue across the table. 'All I was doing was highlighting a serious issue. It's not like I do drugs or mug old ladies or shoplift or anything –'

'All we're saying, Sassy,' Digby says evenly, 'is that a mock hold-up at the local supermarket with a water pistol and a pair of knickers over

[5] I do wish my parents would get their heads round this simple concept when it comes to MY business!

your head might not win your father any votes.'

'So, Dad, you want me to sell out my principles so you can go into politics?'

There's an uneasy stand-off. Mum rolls her eyes in an I-knew-this-would-happen way. Digby looks nervous. Pip tucks into the second cream doughnut. The big grandfather clock in the hall chimes.

'I'm prepared to make it worth your while,' Dad says as the clock falls silent. And I'm just thinking of asking for a rise in my pocket money, when he says something I really am not expecting. 'You behave for the next three weeks, Sassy, and I'll pay for a demo disc.'

I blink as if that will clear my ears. I'm so sure I must have misheard him. I've been trying to get the parentals to cough up for a demo since I was nine.

'Done!' I say before he can regain his sanity. 'For a day in a recording studio, I'll be a perfect daughter.'

Digby stretches out a hand for me to shake. 'It's a deal,' he says with a grin.

'But none of your shenanigans, Sassy.' Dad scowls. 'And I mean it. No run-ins over school uniform. No switching off the school's electricity to give the planet a break. No picketing the car factory in a hedgehog costume. Got it?'

I nod serenely . . .
    angelically . . .
        triumphantly!!!

Then I rush to my room to text Taslima and Cordelia. Sassy Wilde has just passed GO! And she's gonna be a star!

4

I'm in English now. *Romeo and Juliet*. Yawn. Yawn. Muchos muchos boring. If Willie Shakespoke's our greatest playwright ever, thank goodness we don't do the rubbish ones.

Miss Peabody, our teacher – a woman of uncertain years and even more uncertain sanity – is having a ball acting all the parts herself. Cordelia's playing with her tarot cards under her desk. Taslima's doing her freaky asleep-with-her-eyes-open thing, and I'm chewing the end of my Friends of the Forest pencil,[6] gazing dreamily at the back of Magnus's head, when suddenly Miss Peabody wails and collapses in front of the whiteboard. Apparently she's Juliet and she's just found Romeo's body.

Thought: *If I found my one true love lying dead would I kill myself?* No way! But it would make

---

[6] Hand-crafted by peasants from sustainable woodlands in Papua New Guinea.

great publicity and I could write tons of tragic love songs after.

Miss Peabody is dying now. Tragically, noisily. She's so passionate . . . I wonder why she never married. Maybe she just never met the right fella, then her hormones shrivelled up and she became an English teacher. Oh horror! What if that happens to me?

Just then Magnus twists round in his desk and gives me this big smile, and before I know what's happening I kind of smile back, and suddenly these song lyrics flood my brain and I start scribbling furiously, pretending I'm taking notes.

I don't want to be a Juliet to your Romeo
I don't want to be a tragic heroine
I just want to walk a while by your side
I just want to hear you say you are mine.

Cos I lost my heart that day back in class
When we shared a cake, and we shared a laugh
I had my own plans, to fight injustice and greed
But you came along and boy, you're what I need.

I stop scribbling just as the bell goes, shut my jotter quickly and stuff it in my bag – before anyone can see what I've written. I'll do some guitar chords when I get home. I mean, it's good for a singer to show a range and I suppose I should have *one* love song on my demo disc. No one needs to know who I'm singing about, do they?

At lunchtime me, Cordelia and Taslima hang out near the games field. The sun's shining and I'd like to start getting a bit of a tan. I have the kind of sallow skin that looks pale green in winter but eventually turns brown if only I can get out enough.

Cordelia finds a perfect place where I can get the full ultra-violet blast and she can sit under a tree. As a Dolly Goth it would be a disaster for Cordelia if she got a tan. She likes her skin to be pure white, like one of those porcelain dolls. Taslima's naturally cappuccino-coloured, so she sits between us, half in, half out of the shade.

Just then Megan Campbell – yeah, THAT Megan Campbell – appears and homes in on us like a bluebottle to a sticky doughnut. Taslima raises an eyebrow at me. Until recently Megan was under the spell of Hannah Harrison, chewing gum and hanging about outside the chippy in the town centre.

'Hiya!' she squeals, waving her hands excitedly. 'Guess what?'

'Don't tell me!' Cordelia says, putting two fingers to her brow and closing her eyes. 'You're . . . having a . . . party . . . this . . . Friday,' she says like she's receiving a psychic message. 'And you'd . . . love it . . . if . . . we . . . could come.'

'Wow!' Megan's eyes widen. 'That is so freaky! How did you do that?'

'It's a gift.' Cordelia flashes her green eyes enigmatically. I can't help smiling. She was sitting beside Sindi-Sue Shaw last period and, if I had to guess, I'd say Sindi-Sue told her all about it.

'Is it a birthday party?' Taslima asks.

'Nah.' Megan tosses her long blonde hair and it shimmers in the sun. 'Mum wants my new stepbro to meet some of my friends.'

'New stepbro?' Cordelia repeats.

'Yeah,' Megan sighs. 'He came with my mum's new partner. Like a non-optional extra, you know? Like chips with chow mein?'

We exchange a confused look.

'Anyway,' she continues, 'they want him to start school here, but he's not, like, biting. So the wrinklies are going to stay out till midnight so he can meet some peeps. It'd be *so* cool if you guys could come.'

'So who's all going?' Taslima asks. 'Is Hannah going to be there?'

'Nah,' says Megan, 'I don't hang about with Hannah any more.' She throws me a meaningful look, but I make a point of not catching it. 'She was bad news, y'know? So it's mostly folk from our year.' Then she leans in close. 'You know Magnus Menzies, the swim champ?' she whispers, and, despite myself, my heart skips a beat. 'Don't you think he is s-o-o gorgeous? Well, I've just asked him, and –'

'Don't tell me!' Cordelia gasps, closing her eyes dramatically and spreading her fingers wide. 'And . . . he . . . said . . . yes!'

'Yeah! But how did you –?' Confusion clouds Megan's face. 'Oh never mind. Isn't it brilliant? I mean, that boy is so hot!' Megan goes all swoony and something inside me pings, like a tiny alarm going off.

'OK,' Cordelia smiles. 'We'll be there. What time does it start?'

'Any time after eight?' Megan suggests, then stands around like she'd like to chat. But I don't want to. Not unless she's prepared to apologize for the Unforgivable Crime Against Sassy, which she perpetrated when we were in our last year at primary school, and which she has never owned up to and has never said sorry for.[7]

At last Megan simpers, 'See you Friday, then.' And minces off.

[7] Cordelia did suggest I should take revenge. Her advice involved a doll, a shoelace, a pile of pins, a box of matches and a bucket of water. Which, even though I'm furious with Megan, seemed a bit extreme.

As we watch Megan disappear Taslima says quietly, 'There's something about Megan I don't quite get. It's like she's always trying too hard. I think she's quite lonely, actually.'

'Maybe she shouldn't steal from her friends!' I snort.

'Never mind Megan!' Cordelia fixes me with a piercing, don't-lie-to-me-or-I'll-turn-you-into-a-warthog stare. 'Sassy Wilde, I'm only going to ask you once, do you fancy Magnus Menzies or not?'

And I have to be the world's worst ever liar! Even thinking about fibbing makes me feel guilty. And that makes me go pink and grin like a half-witted Cheshire cat.

Taslima looks at my pink face and shakes her head in an exasperated sort of way. 'Why are you in such denial, Sass? It's perfectly normal to fancy the male of the species. And Magnus is pretty much a perfect specimen. So he fancies you – you fancy him. Why not just give in to it?'

I look at her with sad puppy eyes and I know I'm a fool. But I've never had a boyfriend before, and, to be honest, I find the prospect pretty terrifying. Which is daft, because hardly anything scares me. I can pick up spiders, I can perch on the edge of cliffs and dangle off the topmost branches of a tree.

'OK, OK, OK, I suppose I do,' I sigh.

'Well, in that case you *have* to go to Megan's party. Because if you don't, then she'll sink her pretty pink talons into Magnus and you'll end up all heartbroken and tragic like Miss Haversham in that old Dickens book, with cobwebs in your hair and bats flapping in your belfry,' Cordelia warns.

'But I *can't* go to the party,' I protest. 'I've got nothing to wear. And I'm skint.'

Just then a football rockets across in front of us. And who should come running after it – but Magnus. I try to disappear into the grass, but it's no use, it's only a centimetre long. 'Hi, Sassy!' he calls, and gives me a big wave.

Cordelia and Taslima exchange a knowing look. '*You* are going to the party on Friday, Sassy Wilde,' Cordelia says, her green eyes gleaming. 'And no excuses!'

'Yeah,' Taslima giggles. 'Leave it to your fairy godmothers. *We'll* soon find something for you to wear.'

5

After school Cordelia and Taslima come round to my house. I try to put them off, say I'll go to the party in jeans and a T, but they're not having it. Cordelia and Taslima make for my room while I throw together three peanut-butter smoothies with pistachio ice cream topped with rainbow sprinkles, all served up in tall glasses with fluorescent curly straws. Yummy. There's music blaring out of Pip's room, which means she's most probably practising one of her disco-dancing routines.

Digby and Dad are holed up in what Mum now calls the campaign cupboard. Dad calls it his study, but there's no window and not enough room to swing a sausage. They're surrounded by half a rainforest of paper. I've already told Dad what I'd like in his manifesto. I've scribbled suggestions on little Post-it notes and stuck them all over the house – on the fridge, the bathroom mirror, his computer screen. Even on his spectacles. Which got him a bit mad. (He was reading at the time.)

Anyway, I think it's a modest enough list:

- A wormery for every home for disposal of all organic matter (veggie skins, etc.)
- Special exercise bikes linked to generators powering TVs (tackle child obesity and the power crisis in one fell swoop)
- Instant release into the wild of all factory chickens, turkeys and rabbits
- Deportation to the Siberian tundra for anyone who chops down a tree.

By the time I get back upstairs Cordelia and Taslima have tipped my whole wardrobe out on to the bed, shut the curtains, arranged the mirror and set my reading lamp like a spotlight.

'Right,' Cordelia says. 'Let's get down to work!'

I put the smoothies down and stand in front of the mirror. Cordelia circles me, her eyes narrowed in concentration. Taslima chews her bottom lip like she's working out a really difficult maths equation.

Suddenly self-conscious, I try to flatten my curls,[8] as if in some way that makes me look better.

---

[8] Dad says my hair is out of control. Mum says if I don't calm it down she's going to stick an ASBO on it. But I kinda like it. My hair is an expression of my personality. Naturally creative and a bit untamed.

'You're gonna have to change your image,' Cordelia says at last. 'Just for the party.' Then she starts riffling through the leggings, jeans, vest tops and Ts piled on the floor. 'Haven't you anything PINK?' she asks as she chucks aside a black and red rugby shirt. 'You need to look a bit more . . . well . . . vulnerable and needy.'

'But why do I have to be vulnerable and needy?' I whine, in an alarmingly vulnerable and needy way.

'Well,' says Taslima, with her psychologist frown on, 'Magnus needs to think he's your protector. I mean, what's the point in him doing all that swim training, developing such a gorgeous bod, if you look like you could arm-wrestle him to the floor? See, Sassy, you've got to think of him as your knight in shining armour . . .'

'Oh, I can do that easily enough,' I laugh, leaping on to the bed. All mock-dramatic, like Miss Peabody doing Shakespeare, I wave my arms around and wail in a high-pitched voice. 'Look yonder! Who is that handsome knight? Why gallops he so gallantly towards this dark and damnèd tower?'

'Because he's looking for a damsel in distress, so he can rescue her?' Taslima suggests. 'And you, Sassy, have to be that damsel. And damsels do NOT go stomping around at parties wearing saggy old jeans and boggy old Ts!'

'OK!' Cordelia says. 'Chuck all the rejects on the floor, leave the possibles on the bed.'

Five minutes later my entire wardrobe is on the floor.

'I know! I can get exactly what you need!' Taslima squeals, leaping up. 'Jamila has this most gorgeous, slinky little glam dress. It's pale blue. You'd look amazing in it, Sassy. Honestly!' Jamila is Taslima's nineteen-year-old sister. Jaw-droppingly gorgeous. With real boobs and long brown arms and legs. I can't imagine wearing anything Jamila would wear.

'OK, you get that, Tas, and I'll go get my make-up and stuff!' Cordelia grins.

In no time at all my self-appointed fairy godmothers are back in my room with Jamila's dress, Cordelia's hair straighteners and a sackful of make-up. I'm half expecting them to turn Mum's old Saab into a pink stretch limo, and Brewster into a minder in a white tuxedo.

'Nothing that's been tested on animals!' I warn as Cordelia unscrews the top of a bright green tube.

'Listen, little Miss Eco-warrior-babe,' Cordelia scolds playfully, 'I might eat bat-wing stew and fried rats' tails, but I'm not a complete barbarian. Right, first we have to deal with Vesuvius.' And she plonks something damp and stinky on to my third-eye spot.

* * *

Half an hour later a zitless glam chica with straight, glossy hair, long legs and dark kohl-rimmed eyes stares back at me from the mirror.

'Don't look so worried!' Taslima smiles. 'You're not selling out. You're still the same old Sassy on the inside!'

'It's not that.' I sink down on to the edge of the bed. 'Look, guys. You've been great. But I was thinking while you were away getting all the stuff . . . I'm not sure I should go –'

'Why ever not?' Taslima exclaims.

A huge sigh escapes from me. 'It's Megan. It doesn't seem right, you know, going to her party . . . not when I really don't want to be friends with her!'

'Well, *I* don't think you should worry about it,' Cordelia snorts dismissively. 'Megan dissed you back in Primary Seven, didn't she? So, technically, she owes you. So you have every right to go to her party.'

'But what if she thinks I'm friends with her again?' I ask, not quite convinced.

'What Megan thinks doesn't matter,' says Taslima. 'It's what *you* think that counts.'

'Come on, Sassy,' Cordelia says as she packs up her make-up. 'You have to stop holding such a big grudge against Megan. Let it go. It's creating all this negative energy.' She holds her hands up in front of me like I'm firing off bad vibes. 'It's messing up your chakras[9] big time.'

'You both think I should go? I mean, it's not two-faced or anything?'

'You don't have to LOVE Megan to go to her party!' Taslima laughs.

'Anyway, we want you to go!' Cordelia hugs me warmly. 'So you're going, aren't you?'

So I suppose I am.

And I suppose the girls are right. I have to stop feeling so negative about Megan. It's not good for me. I need all my creative energy for my songs. Going to her party will be a *mature* step in the right direction.

As soon as Taslima and Cordelia head for home I give myself the once over in the mirror. From every angle. It feels different being dressed like this. More grown up. And sort of feminine. Quite nice really.

I spend a few more minutes posing in front of the mirror, making sure I can sit down without showing off my knickers – which would totally freak me out – then I leap back into my baggy old jeans, pick up my guitar and sit cross-legged

[9] Chakras, Cordelia says, are the spiritual energy centres of our bodies. According to Cordelia, we each have seven. Personally, I've yet to find any of mine.

on my bed gazing out at the sunlight flickering through the leaves.

Somehow or other my mind drifts to Magnus. I try to imagine his face when he sees me all dressed up.

Then I dig out my English notebook and pick out a few chords and softly sing the lyrics I wrote this afternoon.

> I don't want to be a Juliet to your Romeo
> I don't want to be a tragic heroine

It sounds pretty good. I know I'll need to practise a whole lot more, but I've got this fizzy feeling about it – and I'm glad I took that bite of Magnus's muffin.

And I'm glad that in three weeks I'll be cutting my first demo.

And I'm glad that Cordelia and Taslima are such great mates.

And I'm glad, too, that they're making me go to Megan's party.

6

Biology. And can you believe it? Mr Hemphead[10] has only gone and paired me with Magnus for leaf dissection! Megan looked like she was going to burst a blood vessel. Which, I have to shame-facedly admit, gave me a certain amount of pleasure.

Mr Hemphead passes out the scalpels and the leaves. The curriculum specifies worms, but Old Hemphead's a born-again vegetarian. He says worms and stick insects are a manifestation of the wonder of the universe, so we've got to get by on dissecting non-thinking organisms. And, as a non-violent pacifist, I agree with him. If he'd insisted on worms I would've had to refuse, even though that would've caused all sorts of trouble, which, of course, I've promised I won't get into.

---

[10] Did I say that's not his real name? He's really Mr Hemphill, but no one ever calls him that. Not sure why.

So here I am, inches away from Magnus, trying to concentrate on a leaf. Fortunately my zit has disappeared, frightened off by a dab of what Cordelia claimed was spider spit, but smelled like tea-tree oil.

Magnus gives me the scalpel first. It's really disconcerting standing this close to him. I try to ignore the weird fluttery feeling in my tummy, which, I suppose, must be one of my chakras getting all overexcited. Then I place the scalpel carefully at the top of the leaf and I'm just about to slice down the spine when there's this awful scream from the other side of the lab.

I spin round. Megan's hand is spurting something that looks suspiciously like tomato ketchup.

'Mr Hemphill, sir! Megan's cut herself, sir!' Sindi-Sue shouts. Then all hell breaks loose. Megan wails. Mr Hemphead grabs the first-aid kit from the wall, rushes across the room, sees the blood, turns deathly pale, goes all wibbly-wobbly faint – and keels over!

Megan's howling now like she's amputated her whole arm, and someone's hollering, 'Is there a first aider in here?'

Magnus jumps up and says, 'Yeah, me. I am.'

And he leaves me, leaps over Mr Hemphead – and takes Megan's hand! Next thing he's

dabbing at the blood with cotton wool and anti-
septic, and she's gazing up into his eyes like she's
the Sleeping Beauty and he's the Prince.

And I'm left standing there, gripping my scalpel
really tightly. All of a sudden Taslima appears on
one side of me, and Cordelia on the other, and
before I can say anything they frogmarch me
towards the door.

'What on earth are you doing?' I squeak, as
they push me out into the corridor and slam the
door shut.

'You looked so weird in there!' Cordelia gasps,
at last releasing her grip.

'Like you were going to lunge at Megan!'
Taslima says in a dramatic whisper.

'So we thought it best to get you out –'
Cordelia adds.

'– before you did anything really stupid!'
Taslima finishes.

I look from Cordelia's face to Taslima's.

'Don't be so silly!' I exclaim. 'I'm a pacifist!
I'm hardly going to turn violent over a . . . a . . .
boy.'

'But you did have this mad glint in your eye.
Really scary,' says Cordelia.

'Yeah! Only cos I wanted to turn Megan into
a slimy toad. That's all,' I protest.

'In that case,' Taslima says in an even voice,
'give me the scalpel, Sassy.'

I glance down at my hand. I'm still gripping the scalpel, so tight my knuckles are white.

Carefully I hand it to Taslima. And she heaves a huge sigh of relief.

7

It's Thursday teatime. Party tomorrow! I've got everything under control – hair, make-up, dress. Just one problem. I still haven't asked my darling parentals if I can go.

Truth is, I almost changed my mind after yesterday's little incident. I mean, Magnus did abandon me and go running to Megan's rescue. But, as Taslima pointed out, a trained first aider couldn't possibly have left her to bleed to death all over the floor, could he? It would hardly have been fair on Hilda, the school cleaner, who's downtrodden and suicidal-looking as it is.

What's more, after Megan and Mr Hemphead were carted off to the school nurse, Magnus asked me what I was doing on Friday night. And I said, 'I'm going to Megan's party.' And he said, 'That's great. So am I. See you there, then!'

And even though the thought of seeing Magnus at a party is kind of scary, it's exciting too. He looked so heroic with his shirt all

43

covered in Megan's blood. What's more, Taslima says that the way he went to her rescue shows he has a caring side, which is so important in a chico.

And she figures that having a boyfriend and a singing career are not mutually exclusive.[11] She says a steady relationship with a sensitive and supportive chico might even be a good thing for a star. It would make it so much easier to bat off unwanted advances from fans, for example. And when you came back from a gig he could make you toasted cheese for supper and run a hot soapy bath for you, and tell you how wonderful you are.

I wait patiently while Mum serves the veggie spag bol. If I time it just right Dad will be halfway through shovelling a forkful into his mouth, which means Mum will have said yes before he can swallow and start up his THREE THOUSAND AND ONE QUESTIONS I MUST ASK TO KEEP MY DAUGHTER SAFE.

'Mum, there's a party at Megan's tomorrow. Can I go?' I say, just as Dad's jaws close round his loaded fork.

'Of course, honey bunch,' Mum says absent-mindedly.

[11] Which means, Taslima says, you don't have to choose between them.

44

Then Dad gulps down his pasta and starts to splutter. 'Party? What kind of party?'

'A *party* party,' I explain. 'What other kind of party is there?'

'A political party!' Pip giggles, and I try to kill her with a stare. I am treading delicate territory here. I do not need Pip the Precocious antagonizing my father.

'I mean,' Dad says, 'are you talking all girls – you know, a sleepover kind of scenario – or will there be boys there?'

I clench my teeth. 'It's a party, Dad. I'm a teenager. Remember? So I imagine there will be boys there!'

I look to Mum for support, but Dad's on a roll.

'And alcohol? Because if there's going to be alcohol or drugs or any kind of funny business, then forget it, Sassy! You may be a teenager, but you're only fourteen.'

'Thirteen, Dad,' I correct him.

Dad shrugs. 'OK, thirteen. Anyway, you can't go. I have other plans for you for Friday.'

'Other plans!' I gasp. 'What do you mean you've got other plans? You can stuff your other plans. Mum's said I can go.' And I'm all ready to make a grand foot-stomping exit, complete with slamming door, when, instead of exploding at me, Dad calmly places his fork on his plate and leans back in his chair.

'Well, your mother has forgotten one small fact,' he says smugly. 'It's the Lady Mayor's Buffet to mark the start of the election campaign. All the candidates AND THEIR FAMILIES will be at the town hall.'

Mum slaps her forehead. 'Sorry, Sassy,' she says. 'I completely forgot.'

'Don't I get a say in this?' I demand.

'No, you don't!' Dad snaps, suddenly losing his cool. 'We have an agreement, remember? You're on board with my campaign. For the next three weeks we are one happy and perfect family.'

I stare, incredulous, at our happy and perfect family. Mum's mouth is covered in spag bol, her white blouse spotted with tomato sauce.[12] She looks more like a bulimic vampire than a caring mother.

Pip's sucking in a spaghetti strand in the most disgustingly suggestive manner.

And Dad's doing an impersonation of an irate orang-utan.

'And one last thing,' Dad says as he winds up another huge forkful of spaghetti. 'I'd like you and Pip to wear school uniform.'

That's it! Dad knows I hate school uniform! As

---

[12] Never ever eat spaghetti Bolognese in company. It's impossible to do it politely. Unless of course you're Italian, in which case you have a genetic disposition.

I've pointed out before, the Hitler Youth wore uniforms – and look what that led to!

I storm up to my room and slam the door. I grab my guitar and start to strum furiously. I can feel a new song coming on. An angry, noisy, bitter song. I'm going to call it 'A Cry of Pain in a World of Suffering' and it's going to be the title song of my first album:

WHY MUST MY DAD TRY TO RUIN MY LIFE?
I'M THIRTEEN, I'VE GOT SO MUCH TO GIVE
I WANT TO GO OUT PARTYING
I WANT TO BE MYSELF
I WANT TO DANCE TILL DAWN
NOT SIT HERE ON THIS SHELF –

I'm making such a racket I don't hear Mum tapping at my door. Finally she hammers it so hard it swings open. I scowl as she comes in.

'OK, Sassy,' she says, sitting on the edge of the bed, 'I've negotiated a compromise.'

Huffily I strum my guitar. **STRUM! STRUM! STRUM!**

Mum places a hand over the frets. I've been crying and I know I must look really pitiful – leastways I HOPE I do – cos sometimes, just sometimes, your parents need to know how much they're hurting you.

Mum tugs a hanky from her sleeve and gently

wipes away the tears tumbling down my cheeks.

'The Lady Mayor's Buffet starts at seven. We should be finished by nine. Then we can drop you at Megan's.'

'In my school uniform?' I sniff. 'Thanks but no thanks.'

Mum smiles. 'Put your party gear in a rucksack and change in the back of the car.'

I lick some tears from my top lip and Mum strokes my hair then tucks a curl behind my ear. It makes me feel five years old again. And I can't help but think, *How will I ever be a star if Mum keeps being so sweet?* I mean, all the indie singers I really admire are wild and stroppy and sulky. I can't imagine any of them just calming down and saying, 'That's OK, Mum. Let's hug.'

'When do I get to stay out till?' I sniff moodily. If Mum says ten, then I'll say forget it. Ten would be SO humiliating and make it TOTALLY not worth going.

She thinks for a moment. 'Half eleven,' she says. 'But we'll pick you up after.'

I brighten immediately. 'OK. It's a deal.'

Mum turns at the door. 'I'm really glad you and Megan are talking again,' she says. 'You shouldn't let old grievances fester, Sassy. It's not a good way to live.' Then she's gone.

For a split second I feel bad. Mum's got the

wrong end of the stick about Megan. It's going to take a whole lot more than a measly party invite before I'll forgive her for what she did.

Then it hits me. I'm going to the party! And getting to stay out till half eleven!

Suddenly life seems good again.

8

I hate school uniform.

I have always hated school uniform.

I will always hate school uniform.

When I was in Primary Six I had to sit and copy out this huge mind-numbingly boring bit from the school handbook – *The Importance of School Uniform*.

And all because I turned up in a Greenpeace T-shirt!

I ask you, how can that possibly be educational? Or good for the planet? I grab my pencil and notebook and scribble down some song lines I might work on later.

Uniforms are army gear, and I don't want to
  fight
Don't put me in a uniform, how can that be
  right?
Don't make me wear a shirt, don't make me
  wear a tie

Don't make me wear a skirt, cos I would
  rather die
The world is full of colours, there's more
  than black and white
So let me dress the way I please
In leggings, jeans or dungarees
In lilac, purple, lime or red,
Cos when I wear your uniform
When I wear your uniform
I feel like I
I feel like I
I feel like I am dead!

I chuck the pen and paper down on my desk and curse ever doing the deal with Dad about the demo disc. Cos right now I've got to get into my school uniform so I can be a perfect daughter for my perfect dad to show off his perfect family at the town hall.

Cordelia came round after school to make sure I was all organized for the party later tonight.

Pip was in the hall cupboard, chucking out all sorts of stuff: tennis racquets, skateboards, roller blades, Dad's crampons, Mum's exercise ball, an old hamster cage.

'What on earth are you up to?' I asked as one of Dad's climbing boots flew out and Brewster ran whimpering for cover.

'I can't find my black patent shoes!' Pip sobbed.

Cordelia narrowed her eyes, like she was trying to pick up a psychic signal. Then she disappeared into the back porch and reappeared a few seconds later, dangling Pip's patent shoes.

'Are these what you're looking for, Pip?' she said. Pip crawled out over the piles of junk, her face tear-stained. That's the thing about Pip. Even though she looks like a super-confident Lolitaz doll, she stresses out big style about the tiniest of things.

'So where did you find them?' Pip asked, drying her tears with her sleeve.

'In Brewster's basket.' Cordelia smiled. 'You OK now, Pip?'

Pip gave Cordelia a huge hug and I made a special mint, mango and ice cream smoothie to help restore Pip's equilibrium. Then I dived into the shower, shampooed my hair, rinsed it till it squeaked, then came out wrapped up in my big fluffy robe, a towel wound turban-style around my head.

Once Cordelia had dried my hair, she used her straighteners on it. There was a dreadful smell of burning, and quite a bit of smoke, which she assured me was completely normal. But then singed bats' wings are normal in Cordelia's house.

Pip, happy as a sandboy now with her little patent shoes on, kept rushing in and out of my room, nicking things from Cordelia's make-up bag. I don't know how she does it, but Pip can even make school uniform look naughty. Then

Cordelia headed for home and I packed my rucksack for the party – Jamila's dress, strappy little sandals, mirror, eye shadow, mascara, lip gloss, hairbrush . . . and mints – just in case!

Suddenly the big grandfather clock in the hall starts bonging, which means we should have gone ten minutes ago, and Mum's hollering. 'SASSY! ARE YOU READY? WE'RE ALL WAITING! LET'S GO! NOW!' And Brewster's barking cos he hates all the noise. But I'm still in my bra and knickers, so I leap into my detestable despicable disgusting uniform. (I even have to wear white knee socks. Crimes Against Humanity – that's what those knee socks are!)

By the time we get there the town hall car park is completely full. 'That,' Dad hisses as we park the car on a double yellow about a mile and a half away, 'is because Sassy made us late!'

OK, Father. CHILL! I think, but I keep schtum. I want to make it to the party. *And* I don't want to blow my chances of a demo disc either.

As we set off behind Mum and Dad, Pip takes my hand and grips it really tight.

'You will stay beside me, Sassy?' she whispers. 'You won't leave me?'

'No worries, little sis,' I reassure her as we trot along behind Mum and Dad. 'You stay with me and you'll be OK.' Then I wink at her, like we share a secret.

Ten breathless minutes later we're scurrying up the front steps of the town hall, the oldest and most important building in Strathcarron. As we approach the big oak doors Dad decides he and Mum should make a grand entrance together, with me and Pip bobbing in their wake. The way they've been hyperventilating, I'm expecting some guy in an ancient white wig booming, 'THE LATE MR AND MRS WILDE AND THE TWO LITTLE MISS WILDES.' But there's no one waiting to announce us. We just have to elbow into the main hall, which is huge, with big paintings of Very Important People all round the walls, and so mobbed I don't think anyone would've noticed if we'd been there or not.

When Pip sees all the people she clings to me like a traumatized limpet. Pip does not like crowds.

Dragging her with me, I push my way through to the buffet table. Taslima says we should all make sure we eat before tonight's party. She's read in her *SIZZLE!* (*The mag for girls who wanna be hot!*) that you should never go out partying on an empty stomach. If you do and then you accidentally sip an alcopop or something it'll go straight into your BLOODSTREAM and you might find yourself waking up in a hedge with a sick tummy and a sore head, remembering NOTHING, and at school everyone will nudge each other when you walk past and your photo might appear on some guy's MOBILE and then on someone else's and someone else's and hey presto your life's in TATTERS – and all because you didn't eat a cucumber sandwich before you went out in the first place.

The buffet table is surrounded by parental-type people clutching paper plates and grabbing for food like famished piranhas. Not a pretty sight.

I pull Pip through a tiny gap. Ouch! Some of these older women have sharp elbows. And, I have to say, the underarm odour of the over-forties is far from pleasant. Like Brewster when he's rolled about in cow poo. No kidding! Some of these wrinklies could do with being introduced to a nice bar of organic soap.

I snatch the last plate for me and Pip to share. And that's when I see them. The chicken drum-sticks. Piled high on a silver platter. Pale grey and sweating.

Pip reaches a skinny little arm out to grab one but I get there first. I lift up the whole big silver tray, turn on my heel and reverse through the crush of grey suits and tutting women.

As I look for a sign for the kitchens, an ageing blonde in a turquoise creation stretches her painted talons towards the drumsticks.

'I don't think so!' I exclaim. 'Show some respect for the dead!'

And with that I march off, Pip in tow.

I barge through the swing doors marked STAFF ONLY and follow the sound of clattering dishes until I find the kitchens. A plump woman in a big white apron, surrounded by piles of plates and small mountains of clingfilm – which is NOT biodegradable and will probably end up down some poor seagull's gullet, causing it to suffer a slow and torturous death – smiles cheerily at us.

'Excuse me,' I say, holding up the tray of chicken drumsticks. 'Would you happen to know if these are from free-range chickens?'

'I'm not sure, dearie.' She smiles as she arranges a huge chocolate gateau on a plate. 'I never thought of looking. But the wrappers are all there in the bin, if you'd like to check.'

I set the tray on the worktop and peer into the swing-top bin. There's a big plastic bag, dripping with watery blood, right at the top. I inspect it closely.

CHICKEN DRUMSTICKS.
CATERERS' PACK.
BEST BUMPER VALUE.
CHEEP! CHEEP! CHEEP!

No mention of free range.
Or barn-raised.
Or organic.

Honestly. Just as I suspected.

'Found what you want, dearie?' the woman asks as she offers Pip a creamy spoon to lick clean.

'You wouldn't happen to know who's responsible for ordering these?' I say, once more picking up the tray of drumsticks.

'Well, I suppose that would be the Lady Mayor,' the woman sighs, sprinkling icing sugar over a Victoria sponge. 'I just take them out of the bag, shove them on the trays, stick them in the oven, take them out of the oven, stick them on the plates. Now perhaps you'd like to test one of these for me, precious? Check they're not poisoned?'

She holds out a plate of snowy-white meringues. They look so lovely. All big and fluffy and crumbly, each with a perfect red strawberry stuck into the cream.

And I'm torn. I mean, it would be rude to refuse, wouldn't it?

As I wipe the last sugary crumbs from my mouth, I assure Rosie – that's the cook's name – that her meringues are scrumptious, and that if I keel over dead in five minutes I'll come straight back and tell her, then I pick up the tray of chicken drumsticks to head back to the hall and find the Lady Mayor.

'Can I stay here with you, Rosie?' Pip asks

sweetly. 'In case you need any of the other cakes checked?'

'Course you can, lovie,' Rosie beams. So I leave Pip behind, happily 'helping'. Rosie holds open the door to the corridor and pops an extra strawberry in my mouth, and I find myself thinking how strange it is that some people can be so thoughtless about the chickens and the clingfilm, yet so lovely too, all at once.

Moments later I push back through the swing doors and into the crowded, noisy hall. And I'm wondering how I'm going to find the Lady Mayor when I see a tall woman in a pink suit getting up on to the stage. She's wearing a huge gold chain round her neck like some bling-gone-mad senior citizen.

Everyone stops talking and starts clapping as she approaches the microphone. I wait until the applause dies down, then grab my chance.

'Excuse me!' I say in my loudest voice. In the hushed silence of the cavernous hall it sounds tiny and high-pitched. Everyone turns to stare. 'Are you the Lady Mayor?'

'Indeed I am,' the Lady Mayor smiles. The microphone screeches and a man in a suit rushes to adjust it. For a split second my nerve almost fails. I wonder if I can get away with saying something like, 'Oh, can I have your autograph, please?' then run out and crawl into a hole and never emerge again. But then I think of those chickens. And how they would have suffered, and I know I HAVE to speak out.

'I just wanted to know,' I begin shakily. 'Are YOU responsible for ordering these?' I hold the tray of drumsticks high so everyone can see them. One slides from the pile and tumbles to the floor.

'Ultimately, yes, as this is my buffet, I suppose I am. Is there some sort of problem?' the Lady Mayor asks coolly.

'Well, there is for the chickens!' I blurt. 'I mean, there are . . .' I do a quick guesstimate of the chicken drumsticks on the tray. '. . . eighty-five chicken drumsticks here. That means . . . um . . . forty-two and a half chickens . . . without their legs tonight!'

I take a deep breath and eyeball an obese gentleman holding a half-chewed drumstick. 'Chickens who were forced to live stunted, painful lives cooped up in tiny boxes, chickens who never saw daylight or touched a blade of grass or felt the sun on their feathers, chickens whose young lives were tragically cut short –'

The Lady Mayor comes down from the stage and clicks her way across the hall. Silently, the crowd parts to let her through. Just then I see Dad, over by the side of the stage, his mouth hanging open in horror. I feel my knees start to wobble and I start to wonder – rather late – just how much power a Lady Mayor has? Like, can she order me to be taken to the dungeons? Or publicly flogged? Or sent to a Home For Horrendously Behaved Girls?

Her tall figure click clack click clacks closer and closer and closer. Until at last she looms above me. And then, just when I'm thinking, *That's it, I'm about to be boiled in oil,* she lifts the tray from my trembling hands and says, 'I take it you're offended, my dear. And so am I. Factory chickens are kept in atrocious conditions. I'll speak to the caterers and make sure it doesn't happen again.'

Then she beams down her nostrils and says loudly so everyone can hear, 'It's good to know there are still young people who care enough to make a fuss.'

And suddenly everyone's applauding!

WOW! I SO DID NOT EXPECT THAT!

See, I think as I head for the buffet table so I can get that much-needed cucumber sandwich, *sometimes it pays to stand up for what you believe in.*

Dad obviously does not agree.

He homes in on me from the other side of the hall, his face set in a scowl. *Uh oh,* I think, as he bears down on me, *so this is how a baby seal feels when it sees a hunter coming towards it.* I gulp down a half-chewed mouthful of cucumber sandwich, wondering if it might be my last morsel ever.

'What was all that about?' Dad hisses as he ushers me out and into a darkened cloakroom.

'Chickens have rights too,' I mutter, 'and I am a member of Friends of the Fowl.[13] I have responsibilities.'

'SASSY!' Dad interrupts. 'You agreed you'd behave NORMALLY.'

'But I am behaving normally,' I whimper. 'For me.'

'But I *especially* asked you to lie low!' He throws his hands up in exasperation. 'Don't you understand? You could have completely blown my election chances!'

'Sorrreee!' I mutter, but I guess it comes out less than convincingly, cos Dad's face turns the colour of an overcooked beetroot. Which worries me, you know. If he goes on like this he'll have a heart attack before he's fifty, suddenly keel over and leave Pip and me fatherless, and Mum a Merry Widow.

Dad takes a deep breath in. 'All you had to do was smile politely, look angelic, come across like a well-behaved, well-mannered child. But could you do it? Oh no!'

An uneasy silence descends.

'OK,' he says at last. '*I'm* going back in, but

---

[13] FOF campaigns for better conditions for all farmed birds everywhere.

you're not. *You're* grounded! And as for the demo disc, well, I'll have to think about that.'

I watch, shocked, as Dad disappears back along the dark, shadowy corridor towards the brightly lit hall. As he opens the door the excited babble of voices spills out, then the door swings shut and I'm left alone. I find a dark corner behind the racks of coats and slide down to my hunkers.

A huge sigh escapes from me. I can't believe it – I do the right thing and I get grounded!

Sometimes I wish I didn't care so much about the planet. Sometimes I wish I was like my parents' generation, happy to kill off entire species, to melt the ice caps, to use up all the fuel, to keep animals in inhumane conditions, to chop down acres and acres of forests that took hundreds of years to grow – and not worry about it at all. Just go and have a good night out, an easy life, a guilt-free chicken drumstick.

I glance at my watch. I can just make out its tiny fluorescent hands. It's almost eight. Megan's party will be about to start. She'll be mincing around, all hair-tossingly, eyelash-flutteringly glamorous. And closing in on Magnus.

The cloakroom is gloomy and silent. Eerie even, with all the coats hanging from their pegs, like limp, headless bodies.

Minutes pass slowly. Very slowly. Very, very slowly.

I glance at my watch again. Just after eight. I am utterly miserable.

No party. No Magnus. And I suppose I've blown the demo disc too. Maybe being an eco-warrior demands too big a sacrifice.

Maybe I'm just the saddest, loneliest girl in the entire universe.

9

At last nine o'clock comes, the lights go on in the cloakroom and people start collecting their coats and heading home. One or two even come over and say how much they admire me for speaking up on behalf of the chickens. I smile weakly and don't let on that I kinda wish I'd never done it.

Dad's still bottling his rage as we leave the town hall. He and Mum and Pip walk along in front, arm in arm, while I trail meekly six paces behind.

Apparently Mum had a great time at her first political do. 'Everyone was saying you're a super candidate,' I hear her telling Dad. 'They think you've a great chance of winning.'

Bless Mum. She's doing her best to calm Dad down AND massage his ego before we get to the car. And it's working. He even begins to chuckle a bit. *Yes, yes, yes,* I think, and my heart dares hope a little that he'll change his mind and un-ground me. That maybe, just maybe, little Sassy-Cinders will go to the ball after all!

'What's that thing on the wheel?' Pip says as we approach the car. Something metallic glints under the streetlight. Mum groans.

Dad whooshes up like a dodgy firework.

'I don't believe it!' he splutters. 'We've been clamped.' He turns to me. 'This is YOUR fault. YOU and your SILLY carry-on getting ready. YOU made us late! YOU made me park on a double yellow! I have never EVER in my life, EVER before, parked on a double yellow!'

'Don't blame me!' I snap. 'I don't think we should even have a car! If less people had cars then the North Pole wouldn't be melting and the polar bears wouldn't be disappearing through all the holes in the ice!'

'Shhhhhh . . . Shhhhhhh . . .' Mum's going, looking around anxiously.

'I'll remind you how much you dislike cars next time you ask for a lift,' Dad grunts, crouching down and tugging at the metal clamp as if he thinks he's the Hulk and it's just going to suddenly unlock and come off in his hands.

'For goodness' sake, Angus!' Mum hisses. 'Stand up and calm down!'

Pip slips her hand into mine and grips it tight. She hates any kind of confrontation or anger. She just starts to quiver and grow tinier and tinier. If Pip had to live in a war zone she'd disappear. I put my arm round her shoulder and hug her close.

'We'll get a taxi home and sort out the car in the morning,' Mum says, taking out her mobile and punching in a number.

'Well, Sassy can pay for that – and the parking fine – from her savings!' Dad growls, standing up and straightening his suit.

'Don't worry, Sassy,' Pip whispers. 'You can have all my pocket money.' Which is so sweet of her.

As we climb into the taxi and it speeds us homewards, I fight back the tears. My last chance of going to the party's totally blown now. In fact, I'll be lucky if I'm not grounded, like, forever. And the chorus of my new song whirls round and round inside my head: *Why must my dad try to ruin my life?*

Back home Mum tucks Pip up in bed, then sits Dad down in the living room, puts the TV remote in his hand, his slippers on his feet, and starts making hot chocolate. Cocoa has calming properties, Mum says, so when she's not looking I dollop an extra couple of spoonfuls into Dad's mug.

'I'm sorry about the party,' Mum whispers to me in the kitchen.

'It doesn't matter,' I lie. 'I'm tired. I'm going to bed.'

'Good idea.' Mum smiles sadly. 'Tomorrow's a fresh day. Night-night, honey.' She gives me a hug and a kiss, then I wander up to my room, telling myself all the reasons why it's actually BRILLIANT that I'm not going to Megan's party.

1. I don't like Megan anyway.

I'm in my room and struggling to come up with number two when my mobile buzzes. I rummage to the bottom of my backpack, chucking Jamila's dress on to the bed. Three missed messages from Cordelia.

Message one: Magnus here! Woo hoo! Where r u? xxx
Message two: Come kwik. ☺
Message three: SOS! Megan closing in on Magnus! Hurry up!!!!!

I take my stupid school uniform off and chuck it on the floor. I'm just about to stamp on it for good measure when my eye is drawn to the little pale blue glam dress, lying crumpled and sad on the bed. I pick it up and smooth it. Before I know what's happening the dress is over my head and my hand is zipping it up!

And all the time a little voice is nipping at my ear. 'Why should you have to miss the party, Sassy, just because your dad was stupid enough to park on a double yellow?'

I put some extra liner round my eyes, add a touch of mascara, a weensy bit of lip gloss, then stare at my reflection. 'It would be such a waste to just go to sleep now . . . wouldn't it?' says the little voice.

Just then I hear the parentals pass on their way to bed. Dad yawns loudly. The hot-choccy over-dose taking effect, I hope.

I put some sounds on low. Then, ever so quietly, I open my bedroom window. My room's on the first floor, but since I was about seven I've used the tree outside as an emergency exit. I've prac-tised lots of times. In case of nuclear war, tsunamis, earthquakes or whatever.

I hitch my dress up and ease myself on to the thick branch that reaches right over to the house, then on all fours I edge along it. Quickly and easily I scramble down through the branches, then keeping to the shadows I dash across the garden. Before I slip through the gate I glance back up at the house. Just in time to see Mum and Dad's light clicking out.

10

Megan's is only five minutes from mine if you take the shortcut through Bluebell Wood.

When we were little, me and Megan used to meet in the wood nearly every day and play for hours. All sorts of adventures. She'd be the beautiful Sky Child captured by the Grumpits from Middle Earth, and I'd be Zara, Warrior Princess. She'd be tied to a tree courtesy of Mum's washing line, and I'd come galloping up on my magical unicorn, Xianthon, brandishing my laser sword, rushing to her rescue.

One summer we took all our My Little Ponies camping in a den under the rhododendron bushes. We left them there overnight. Next day we couldn't remember where. It was winter before we found them, smothered in dead leaves, spider-webs and bird droppings. We couldn't play with them again, so we gave them a decent burial and marked the spot with a little pink cross with all their names written on in sparkly glitter pen. It was very moving.

I stop where the path leaves the lighted road and dips into the darkness of Bluebell Wood. If I dashed through I'd get to the party quicker. Three minutes max and I'd be there.

But though I love the wood during the day – when the sun dapples through the leaves and the air's all full of birdsong and the little squirrels go leaping through the high branches, and if you sit really quiet and still you might even see a fox – at night the woods are dark and scary. There might be a mad axe-man or a mass murderer lurking in the shadows. And much as I want to be a great singer and everyone knows that dying young has always been a sure-fire career move – I really need to have an album out first . . .

While these crazy thoughts bounce through my head my legs carry me along the brightly lit roads. Then whaddaya know! I'm standing outside Megan's house, trying to get my breathing to slow. All the curtains have been pulled shut, but the windows are open and the boom boom boom of music, the excited babble of voices, the occasional squeal of laughter, spill out into the cool night air.

I tug my dress down, smooth my hair and walk up the path.

I ring the front-door bell but no one answers, and I'm just wondering whether to bang on a window when something hits the top of my head.

'Ouch!' I squeal, spinning round, eyes searching the dark garden. 'What was that?'

'A nut. Thought you might like one,' a voice says somewhere above me. I look up into the branches of the only tree, but all I see is darkness. Suddenly the front door opens and light and noise flood out.

'Sassy! Great!' Megan flaps her arms like she's really pleased to see me, then drags me inside. Another nut bounces off the back of my head.

'Get lost, Twig!' Megan hollers into the dark, and slams the door.

'Twig?' I ask. 'Who's Twig?'

'My new stepbro.' Megan flutters her eyelashes in a long-suffering way. 'Ignore him. He's weird.'

Cordelia and Taslima give me a great big hug when at last I find them in the darkened living room. The place is heaving. I guess Megan must have got carried away with her invite list!

In the corner Sindi-Sue is draped over an armchair. A herd of boys drool over her like she's an ice-cream sundae with a cherry on top.

Magnus, thank goodness, is not among them. Sindi-Sue gives me a little fluttery-fingered wave and mouths, 'Wow! You look great!' Which instantly makes me wish I was in my old jeans and T, cos I really don't want to be on Sindi-Sue's 'approved' list.

The music in the living room's ear-bleedingly loud and I can't see Magnus anywhere, so I grab Cordelia's arm and she grabs Taslima and together we push through the mass of dancing bodies, out into the hall.

And that's when this little bubble of fear starts to grow inside my chest. I mean, only a week ago I promised Dad I'd behave, not get into any trouble, be a perfect daughter.

And I know maybe I should've thought of that before I climbed out of the window, but I was so annoyed with Dad and the little voice in my head made it seem like such a good idea: 'Sneak out to the party, dazzle Magnus, get him to walk you home, climb back in the window – hey presto – morning!'

Clinging to each other so we don't get separated, me, Cordelia and Taslima push our way through the hall and into the dining room, where Megan says we'll find some drinks. A group of older boys are lounging by the open patio doors, slugging from what look like bottles of lager. I can't imagine what those boys are even doing here. I'm sure Megan doesn't know them.

As we shove our way through to the table where all the juice and crisps and goodies are laid out there's a crash and a flash as someone accidentally knocks over a table lamp. A big cheer goes up and the bubble of fear inside my chest gets bigger and bigger, pushing against

72

my lungs, filling up with all kinds of horrible thoughts.

What if the neighbours call the police because of all the noise? What if they suddenly raid the party? What if I get flung into the back of a police van and taken to the police station and Dad gets called and tomorrow's headlines scream:

OUT-OF-CONTROL TEENS – CANDIDATE'S DAUGHTER ARRESTED!

'I'll get the juice,' Taslima giggles into my ear. She looks lovely tonight, a pale yellow top showing off her cinnamon skin, her eyes huge and dark as coffee beans. 'You grab some goodies.'

She elbows her way in and fills three plastic cups with apple juice. I grab a paper bowl and pile handfuls of crisps and nuts and marshmallows and strawberry shoelaces and cheese strings in it, then we nudge our way towards the hall, where it's quieter. Cordelia looks knockout in a black tutu, scarlet tights and black over-the-knee socks with little silver stars on. Boys keep turning and staring at her.

At last we find a space halfway up the stairs. Taslima gives me a cup of juice and it's so full I have to sip it right away to stop it spilling. Then Cordelia and Taslima are about to update me on what I've missed so far when Mad Midge

Murphy[14] goes sliding down the banister, shouting, 'Hiyaz, girlz,' then leaps off at the bottom and takes a dramatic bow before disappearing into the toilet.

'So tell me everything!' I say excitedly, taking a sip from the juice.

'Megan has been trying to corner Magnus . . .' Cordelia gasps, waving her hands dramatically. 'But he keeps making excuses to get away from her.'

'I was chatting to him for a few minutes,' Taslima adds. 'And he asked if you were coming. And I said yes. And he said *Great!* and couldn't stop grinning!'

My heart does this little double-flip thing like a tiny Olympic gymnast and – KAPOW – the bubble of fear, which was all but stopping me from breathing a few minutes ago, bursts and my head's thinking, *Oh yes, yes, yes, please, please, please . . .*

. . . when the living-room door swings open and Megan emerges, laughing, into the hallway. Dragging Magnus.

We sit, frozen, like kids watching the grown-ups through the banisters, as Megan throws her arms

---

[14] He's not called Mad Midge for nothing. He once ran away from home and lived in a wheelie bin for three days.

74

round his neck and their mouths lock in a passionate kiss.

Inside my head there's this loud noise, like a great iron door clanging shut. My fist tightens round the paper cup, and the juice squishes up – and spills all down the front of my pale blue dress, making this huge, dark, sticky stain.

Which, in a silly way, I'm quite glad about. Cos it gives me the perfect excuse to go home early.

11

They say you can't really sing a love song till you've had your heart broken. That's what I'm thinking as I shut the door of Megan's house.

Of course, when I was dabbing at Jamila's dress with a towel in the kitchen, I'd told Cordelia and Taslima I was ABSOLUTELY TOTALLY ABSOTUTALLY fine about the Magnus/Megan thing.

'Really, I'm OK,' I'd insisted. 'Like I said before, I don't have time for a boyfriend. Single suits me. Honest! But I think I'll go home anyway. Get out of this dress.'

Just then Midge Murphy came leaping in to tell us that a new game of Spin the Bottle was starting up in the living room. It was so obvious he desperately wanted Cordelia to be in it![15]

'We need to walk Sassy home,' Cordelia said loyally, and Midge's face crumpled.

---

[15] Poor boy must have a death wish!

'Look, I'll be fine!' I insisted, forcing a laugh. 'Don't fuss! It's only a five-minute walk. Phone me tomorrow and tell me everything!'

Before they could protest, I was gone.

As I walk down the garden path all the hurt and disappointment I've been suppressing starts to push up inside me. I grit my teeth and give myself a firm talking to. *You're a winner, Sassy. You're gonna cut a demo and it's gonna take the world by storm and then Magnus will be sorry.*

Suddenly something cracks my skull. A nut! I spin on my heel and glower into the darkness. 'DO THAT AGAIN, PSYCHO,' I scream, letting all my anger and frustration out in one almighty whoosh, 'AND YOU'RE DEAD MEAT!'

Then I storm off into the street.

I can't believe I just said *dead meat*! How could I say that? I mean, I'm a vegetarian. And a pacifist. Whether animal or human, I cannot condone reducing anyone to the status of dead meat! Secretly, inwardly, I blame Megan. And Magnus. This is insufferable. They are turning me into a monster.

As I stride away from Megan's house my heart thumps its fists against my ribcage. Then I remember something Taslima once said: *If you feel panicky try to breathe through your heels.* I know it sounds silly, and I don't exactly understand what she means, but I concentrate on pulling my breath right up from my heels – and miraculously I start to feel more calm.

At last my heartbeat settles and my pace slows. I look up at the sky. There's a lovely silvery moon tonight. And suddenly, unexpectedly, whole bucketfuls of tears start streaming down my cheeks. Because it would've been so perfect walking home with Magnus. We could've stopped at the end of my road and maybe I would have let him kiss me. And it would have been my first kiss – ever!

Just then a cloud floats across the moon, the streetlamp nearest me flickers out and I'm plunged into darkness. And I don't know if it's because I'm dressed up in a silly little dress and silly little sandals like the kind of girl who's all feminine and vulnerable, but I start to feel really feminine and vulnerable.

A few steps further on, I stumble on a loose paving slab, my ankle twists and I fall clumsily.

Suddenly a voice behind me says, 'Are you OK?'

Startled, I look up.

'Don't panic! It's only me. Twig. Megan's stepbro.'

And I'm just thinking, *Oh no, it's the weird nut-throwing psycho*, when he grips my hand and heaves me to my feet.

'You OK?' he asks again.

'Of course I'm OK,' I snap, tugging my hand free. Then I start limping off along the pavement. His footsteps follow me. Angrily I spin round.

'Do you mind? I'm going home. Alone. And I do NOT need an escort.'

'Well, I think you do,' he says, and next minute he's right beside me again.

'You've been crying, haven't you?' he asks, and his voice is gentle.

'I twisted my ankle, that's all.' I sniff. 'It's cool.'

'You shouldn't be walking home on your own,' he says. 'You never know who you might meet.'

'Look, I'm going home,' I say firmly, trying not to hobble.

'I know,' he says. 'Let me walk you.'

'Don't bother. I can look after myself.'

He looks me up and down, taking in my tear-stained face, my tiny glam dress. I sniff again and wipe my cheeks with the back of my hand.

'I'm fine. Honestly.'

'Whatever,' he says, and disappears off into the darkness.

I limp off along the path, confused. What kind of chico leaves a damsel in distress to walk home alone late at night?

Then it hits me. Maybe it's just me! Maybe even in a glam dress with a twisted ankle and a tear-stained face I still look like some Amazon-Warrior-Lara-Croft-type who could karate chop a brick at twenty paces and who no self-respecting chico would dare to come near.

I am so glad to reach my house at last. I limp round to the back garden, keeping to the shadows, then start climbing up the tree to get back in. I'm about to crawl along the branch that leads to my window when the dress snags and there's this really loud ripping sound. I freeze, terrified my parents might have heard.

Almost immediately the stair light flashes on and my heart plummets. This has to be the worst night of my life. I've lost Magnus to Megan, and now Dad is going to kill me.

I close my eyes and brace myself for Dad's shout. But all I hear is the sound of someone peeing, then the flush of the toilet! The stair light flicks off and the house falls still again. Attacked by a sudden fit of giggles I almost fall out of the tree.

Five minutes later I'm snuggled down under my duvet with Tiny Ted tucked in beside me, and for some reason I'm not sobbing my heart out.

So maybe it's not broken after all.

Only slightly cracked.

I fall asleep not quite able to work out why . . .

12

Guess what? Apparently my little outburst at the Lady Mayor's Buffet last night raised Dad's profile as a candidate! Two radio stations and one of the local papers have been in touch already, wanting to interview him about his campaign.

Digby's delighted. He says they could never have got so much exposure on their own. It's worth a thousand election leaflets, Digby says. And they've even had people calling up this morning offering to help with mail-outs and stuff. As a reward Digby bought me a Phoenix Macleod CD. Which is really cool, cos Phoenix Macleod writes and sings his own songs just like me.

The bad news is that the Lady Mayor has announced that she too is going to stand as a parliamentary candidate. That, says Digby, makes things all the more difficult for a newcomer like Dad.

Mum sorted out the car. She had to pay a fifty-pound fine to get it back. More than it's worth, Dad moaned, but Digby says the campaign fund will foot the bill for that and the taxi. So Pip can keep her pocket money and Agnes, my adopted donkey, will have her oats provided for another few months.

What's more, Dad says that after careful consideration – and some campaigning on my behalf by Mum, Pip and Digby – he's decided that the deal for my demo disc still stands!

Pip cheers and does a silly boogie dance around the kitchen. 'You can be all happy again now, Sassy,' she says, grinning. 'Everything's worked out OK!'

I hug her and force a big smile. I don't want to tell Pip about all the other things that are bothering me – like Magnus kissing Megan and me coming home all upset. She might pretend to be all grown up, but she's actually sweet and innocent at heart.

So now I'm up in my room, strumming my guitar, making myself think of all the reasons I have to be happy. Like Cordelia and Taslima, who are the best friends any girl could wish for. And how I'm gonna cut a demo disc – in just three weeks' time – when I come to a momentous decision, which, I think, will affect the course of the rest of my life.

I am going to forget all about Magnus. Forever.

Suddenly I feel so much better. I play this happy little tune. I smile at myself in the mirror.

When – KAPOW! – this bit of my brain I don't have any control over starts to think about Magnus again. And a big black cloud descends. And my reflection stops smiling back at me. And I feel all tearful and hurt.

I am Sassy Wilde, I remind myself sharply. *I refuse to get all weepy over a boy!* I strum my guitar hard a few times, then my head starts filling up with lyrics for a new song, 'My Bungee-jumping Heart', about how I'm up one minute and down the next.

I scribble the lyrics into a notebook and hope that'll be the end of it.

I will be so glad when I'm no longer a teen and all this silly hormone stuff stops. Then I can just get on with my life.

I'm in the kitchen just finishing off one of Mum's fab Scotch drop pancakes with maple syrup – and thinking about how easy it would be to get fat if you were always getting your heart broken, cos you most def do feel better when you're tucking into something sweet and sticky – when Cordelia materializes on the doorstep.

I can tell from the minute Cordelia comes into the kitchen that she's got something she's dying to tell me. She kinda hops about like a little girl desperate for the loo. And I have this awful moment when Mum says, 'So did you have a good time at Megan's, Cordelia?' And I think Cordelia's going to forget that I wasn't supposed to be there and put her tiny red-shoed foot in it, but at the last minute she tunes into the thought vibes I'm firing across the kitchen, and she says, 'Oh, it was OK. Nothing special. But we did all miss Sassy.'

Phew! Moments later we dash out of the door and go whispering to the old swing at the bottom of the back garden. Mum shakes her head after us, saying, 'Girls!' in an exasperated, happy way.

'You'll never guess what happened right after you left,' Cordelia gasps as soon as we're out of earshot. 'Magnus kept trying to get away from Megan. I mean he obviously did NOT want to be with her.'

'Well, why was he kissing her, then?' I ask, surprised.

'Oh, they were playing Spin the Bottle,' Cordelia explains. 'That was just a dare! But afterwards she kept throwing herself at him . . .' She pauses, her eyes wide. 'So he walked out! And she stormed upstairs.'

Cordelia perches on the little kiddy-swing. 'Like we weren't much bothered cos that's SO like Megan. Anyway a crowd of us all piled out to the back garden cos Beano said he'd seen a shooting star. Then someone said that Megan had locked herself in her mum's en suite bathroom and Sindi-Sue went all *Omigod I hope she's all right!'*

Cordelia does a funny impersonation of Sindi-Sue in a panic, and I smile.

'So she went rushing off and started banging on the door, telling her to open it and not do anything stupid. Course we weren't there – like we were still out in the garden – but APPARENTLY Sindi-Sue was getting really hysterical so this big guy forced it open! And they found Megan . . . sitting on the floor . . . all tear-stained with these little brown bottles all around her –'

'You mean she . . .' I gasp.

'Like I said,' Cordelia sighs, 'we were in the garden staring up at the sky. First thing we knew about it all was when this ambulance came flying into the street, blue lights flashing and everything. Course we all rushed round to see what was up. Just in time to see Megan getting wheeled away on a stretcher, her face all ghostly white!'

I stare at Cordelia, and I swear my mouth is hanging so wide open you could float a great blue whale straight in. I mean, how sad and mixed up do you have to be to get so upset about a boy?

'And is Megan OK?' I ask at last, a sick feeling tightening its fist round my tummy.

'I really don't know.' Cordelia frowns. 'It wasn't like we could stay around to find out. But I had this dream last night.' Her voice goes mystic and distant. 'And it was like I saw her in hospital, in intensive care, just lying there, staring.'

Cordelia's gone now and I'm up in my room again, strumming my guitar.

I think about Megan for a while, and I feel really, really sorry for her. Then my thoughts drift to what Cordelia said about Magnus.

Apparently he went up to her just minutes after I left and asked where I was. And Cordelia lied and said I'd gone home cos I was tired, and he said, 'Well, that's a shame, cos I saw her come in and she was looking really cool. She should wear her hair straight more often.'

Cordelia watched me carefully as she told me this. I felt my colour rise.

'Sassy!' She grinned wickedly. 'You do still fancy him, don't you?'

'Well, yeah,' I admitted. 'If there's nothing between him and Megan.'

I pick out a few chords and try to make up a new song – about a boy who swims like a dolphin. But I can't block out this image of Megan all tubed up, lying on a hospital bed, a little machine going *beep beep beep* above her, and I feel so bad.

I mean, I've always wanted revenge for her

Crime Against Sassy, but I never wanted her to end up in hospital. I'm not that vengeful. A little accident, probably involving her hair, which she is really, really vain about – like the hairdresser messing up and her coming out with it luminous green, oh and totally frizzy. *That* was the worst I ever wished for.

The thing is me and Megan go way back. We met at nursery. At the water-play basin. I'd just put Diver Dan on top of his diving board and she immediately whacked him into the water, which every three-year-old knows is just not acceptable.

Anyway I clobbered her and made her nose bleed and she scratched me and made my hand bleed and all the water went red and swirly and she was howling and I was howling and then we were Best Friends forever. Blood Sisters even.

Until Primary Seven, that is.

Suddenly my mobile beeps and I dive for it. It's Taslima. And guess what? Megan phoned Taslima half an hour ago, and she's absolutely fine! This big whoosh of relief rockets up through me.

According to Megan, it was all a silly misunderstanding. She'd eaten nothing but boiled eggs for three whole days so she could get into her fave dress for the party, and then she'd been SO ravenous she'd gobbled a bumper bag of spicy salsa crisps and a whole pile of strawberry laces – not to mention a couple of cheese strings – then suddenly she had this HUGE tummy ache, so she'd gone into her mum's bathroom and was trying to get some Tummy Soothers from the medicine cabinet when she went all dizzy and knocked all her mum's pill bottles on to the floor and that's when someone burst the door open and everyone freaked out completely and next thing she knew she was in hospital trying to convince them not to pump her stomach. What a complete and totally-blotally FIASCO!

I'm so glad she's OK. I really did not want her to die.

Before she rings off, Taslima asks if I'm still feeling OK, you know, about the Magnus thing. And I say it's cool, which it is. Cos compared to dying, getting juice spilled over your dress and your heart slightly cracked is nothing. Taslima says it is so obvious Magnus and me should be together, and that the path of true love never runs smooth. She says Megan was just a little bump along the way.

Then Taslima has to go cos she's used up all her free minutes, so I chuck my mobile on the bed, pick my guitar up again and try an F chord.

When I was first learning to play my fingers hurt so much I didn't think I was ever going to overcome the pain of the metal strings cutting into them. I had to soak my fingertips in vinegar[16] to harden them up, and now it hardly bothers me at all.

I put the F chord together with an A minor and a D, which is kind of tricky, and I start to hum along to it. Then, once I've got the rhythm going, I start to sing.

> Oh why can't people be more like dolphins?
> A dolphin's face always meets you grinning
> A dolphin is free – he's got no need to kill
> A dolphin is happy – he swims for the thrill.
>
> A dolphin just wants to live in the ocean
> He doesn't pollute, he ain't got no notion
> Of nuclear bombs and nuclear fusion
> Or killing, or wars, or starting aggression.

And I'm really getting it together and enjoying it, so I start belting it out:

> Oh why can't people be more like dolphins?
> A dolphin's face always meets you grinning
> He don't need no factories pumping out smoke
> He don't need no bombs, he doesn't kill folk.

[16] I have read some not very savoury types use their pee! Yuck! I do NOT think so.

He don't build no roads, he don't poison the air
And we're killing his world, acting like we don't
 care
It makes me so sad, it makes me so mad
The planet's in crisis, it's us are to blame.

And in my head I'm playing at Glastonbury and the audience is totally silent as I go into the last verse.

Oh why can't people be more like dolphins?
I don't wanna be human, I can't stand the shame
But what can I do, 'cept stand up and sing
Don't ruin our world. No! Not in my name!

Then there's this rapturous applause and they're whooping and hollering and I see this gorgeous chico down near the front of the crowd – and it's Magnus – so I smile and wave him up on to the stage . . .

When I realize I'm ACTUALLY in my bedroom.

But there IS applause.

Someone IS clapping.

Someone sitting in the branches of the tree – of MY tree – outside MY window. It's the boy from last night! Megan's stepbro. Twig.

Suddenly he sees me seeing him, and I'm about to shout something really rude when he disappears. I rush over to the window just fast enough to see him legging it across the lawn and leaping the wall at the far end of the garden. Poor Brewster is lolloping around in the flowerbed, sniffing the air, confused.

And I'm confused too. I should be angry. Furious, even. I mean, that is TOTALLY not on, sitting outside a girl's bedroom window, staring in!

No wonder Megan said he was weird. He must have followed me all the way home last night and watched me climb in through my window in my eensy-weensy dress. (Blushblushblush!)

I shut the curtains. Just in case he's daft enough to come back. Then I pick my guitar up and start strumming again. I try to conjure up the scene with me and Magnus at Glastonbury. I was having such a good time.

But every time I wave Magnus up on to the stage, Megan's stepbro barges on in front of him.

I give in and set the guitar on its stand. My tummy's rumbly-grumbly again, demanding attention. There's a lovely smell floating up from the kitchen. I guess Mum's having one of her mad baking days. I'm off to see what I can nick.

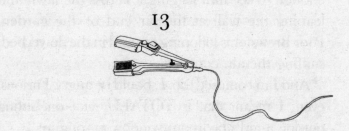

13

All weekend I waited for today, Monday, cos I really wanted to see if Magnus might say something to me about the party. And guess what? He wasn't even at school.

Mr Lovelace, the swim coach, whisked him off first thing to time trials in Edinburgh – for the Scotland junior team!

It doesn't totally surprise me, though, because he really is a brilliant swimmer. Sometimes we have these interschool galas and Cordelia and Taslima and me go along to watch and Magnus beats everyone easy every time. To be honest, I think that's maybe when I first fell for him. Long before the original muffin incident. It was his butterfly stroke that did it. Made him look like a dolphin. And, let's face it, dolphins have to be the most attractive creatures in the ENTIRE universe (apart from polar bears, and seal cubs, and baby pandas, of course).

* * *

It's Monday night now and Dad and Digby have gone to the printers to pick up the election leaflets and posters. I insisted they were all produced on recycled, unbleached paper to cause as little damage to the environment as possible, and Dad agreed.

Last week Dad got a publicity photo taken especially for the campaign. Digby says his face will be stuck up on lamp posts all around the town. I'm hoping no one at school will make the connection between the dodgy guy swinging from the lamp posts and me. But why should they? I look nothing like my dad. For starters I don't have hairs growing out of my ears.

I let Miss Peabody talk me into standing in a mock election in English tomorrow, so now I've got to draw up a political manifesto and prepare a speech. I'm standing for the Save Our Planet Party. SOPP for short. Megan's standing against me. For the GTPWTW Party. Which, as Cordelia pointed out, is totally unpronounceable and impossible to remember. Megan says it stands for Give The People What They Want.

The thing about SOPP is it's specifically for young people. In my opinion – which is what Miss Peabody says I've got to give in class tomorrow – people old enough to vote don't care about the planet or the environment cos it's not going to be their problem, is it? They're all going to die soon anyway.

So I intend highlighting the gross irresponsibility of the older generations, i.e. anyone over the age of eighteen.

Take, for example, the question of disposable nappies. In the UK alone babies get through 8 million a day! Disgusting or what? I mean, what is Britain going to look like in another fifty years? Just counting from today, at least another 146,000 million baby nappies will have been tipped into landfill sites. Not to mention the giant incontinence nappies from the huge numbers of grand-parentals who'll all be turning gaga. Just think what that will add to the nappy mountain!

What's more, our parentals and grand-parentals haven't just messed up Planet Earth, they've even dumped litter all over outer space! Old rockets, satellites, motors, nuts, bolts. There's even a baseball glove some stupid astronaut dropped, circling around up there. And a golf ball.

And goodness knows what junk they've dumped in the bottom of the ocean. It used to be the worst you'd get was the odd shipwreck loaded with gold doubloons and sunken treasures. But now everything and anything gets chucked in the sea. I mean, did you know that ladies' sanitary protection (I'm gonna leave that bit out of tomorrow's speech, of course) takes two seconds to flush down the loo, but zillions of years to decompose?

I mean, if I was a dolphin, which, believe me, sometimes I'd much rather be, I would be absolutely furious!

Yet parents go on a rant yelling at us to tidy our ROOMS, when they're gonna leave the WHOLE PLANET in a TOTAL MESS when they pop their clogs.

And we won't be able to do a thing about it. Just huddle in what's left of our towns, hoping the hurricanes and tsunamis won't get us.

By the time I've put the finishing touches to my speech, I'm totally exhausted. And a nervous wreck.

Sometimes I think I'm more eco-worrier-babe than eco-warrior-babe. It keeps me awake at night worrying about the planet, global warming, dying elephants, starving children, and everything.

So I have a lovely hot bath then Pip comes into my bed for a while and I read her her fave bedtime story from when she was tiny – *Princess Popsicle and the Naughty Peanut*.

Then I get tucked up with Tiny Ted under my duvet and try to think of good things, happy things. Like dolphins . . . and Magnus.

I'm going to get up extra early tomorrow. Magnus should be back. And I've decided to straighten my hair before school.

* * *

My alarm beeps at six thirty, which is inhumanly early, but even so I positively ping out of bed and into the shower.

Next I need to straighten my hair. A strictly temporary measure till Magnus gets to know me better and grows to love its natural curliness.

Of course, I don't personally OWN straighteners, on account of the contribution they make to global warming,[17] but fortunately my incredibly vain little sis does.

Pip's still asleep, so I creep into her room in the half dark. I don't often go into Pip's room. The Lolitaz poster smouldering on the door makes me want to run screaming in the opposite direction. Do you know there's a Lolitaz for every girly fantasy you can imagine? Drama Queen Lolitaz, Clubbing Lolitaz, Biker Girl Lolitaz. Each one as ugly as the other. But Pip loves them. She's wheedled nine dolls out of Mum and Dad already, even though they don't approve of them.

I tiptoe across her room, almost breaking my leg on my old pogo stick. What on earth is that doing in here? It's not the kind of thing you can boing on inside the house without risking crashing through the floor.

[17] I mean, if you put all the heat together of all the hair straighteners switched on in the world you could probably power a small country.

I'm just about to unplug her straighteners and creep back out when Pip makes this little sighing sound and turns over. Her bed is like a big sugary pink satin marshmallow. It would give me nightmares to sleep in it. Sometimes I think they gave Mum the wrong little bundle at the maternity hospital. Pip is so into girly, frilly things.

I stand perfectly still and watch her for a few moments. She's got her thumb in her mouth and her chubby little face is all cherubic and childish. Pip's eyelids flutter, and a tiny smile twitches at the corners of her mouth, like she's having a lovely dream. I hope she is. And I hope she stops trying to grow up so fast. There's a lot to be said for being nine. She's still a pheromone-free zone. She doesn't need to worry about boys, or bra size.

Or, for that matter, bungee-jumping hearts.

14

WOW! My hair looks so cool. I can't believe how much longer and shinier it becomes when it's straightened. (On the downside, it does make me look like every other girl at school, but, you know, I think I could really get used to it.) It's such a bummer it's not naturally straight. I hope my sproglets inherit Magnus's hair rather than mine.[18]

I'm first in the kitchen this morning. I can hear Dad yodelling in the shower and Mum wandering around her bedroom bumping into things. She's as blind as a new-born kitten till she puts her contacts in. As a special treat for Mum I pop the kettle on.

Then I throw some fruit into the smoothie

[18] Yikes! Where did that thought come from? This whole hormone thing is getting a bit frightening. I don't even know if I want to have sproglets. Ever. With or without hair. I mean, an adopted donkey is already quite a responsibility.

maker. Sassy's Early Morning Wake-up Special – banana, kiwi and yoghurt, with a dollop of honey.

I'm just about to take a first slurp when I see one of Dad's new election leaflets lying on the table. Oh my gosh-oh-golly-glumpit! The mug-shot on the front is even worse than I feared. You can make out these little nostril hairs he must have missed when he shaved. It looks like he's got this tiny moustache – scarily like Adolf Hitler!

His name – half of which I unfortunately have to share with him – is in big bold letters across the top.

ANGUS WILDE. A FAMILY MAN WITH FAMILY VALUES.

I'm still hoping no one knows he's related to me. Especially Hannah Harrison, who would just love to make my life a misery.

And I'm just thinking how weird it is, you know, that Dad might end up being a member of parlia-ment, when absent-mindedly I flick the leaflet open.

CATASTROPHE!

A photo of a small child in her bath. Naked. And underneath: *Angus Wilde, doting father, bathes his daughter.*

Just as I open my mouth to scream, Dad bounces into the kitchen.

He halts mid-yodel and looks startled.

'How could you?' I blurt. 'You have ruined my life!' I sob, tossing the leaflet on to the table.

Dad picks up the leaflet and peers at it.

'Sorry, Sassy,' he says. 'I'm not with you.'

'Don't you see? I can never go out in public again,' I scream as Mum comes in, blinking. 'Everyone's going to tease me stupid!'

'What on earth's going on?' Mum asks blearily. 'I thought somebody was being murdered.'

I grab the leaflet from Dad's hand and thrust it under her short-sighted nose. 'See what Dad's done!' I wail. 'That's it! I can't ever go to school again. Ever.'

Mum peers at the photo. 'For goodness' sake, Sassy. It's only an old baby photo.'

'Yes, Mum! NUDE! Of ME! NAKED! Like . . . like . . . a Page-Three Pin-up or something!'

'So that's what the problem is!' Dad says at last. 'But that's Pip in the photo, isn't it?'

I fire him a filthy look. 'That's ME, Dad. What kind of doting father are you? It looks nothing like Pip.'

'To be fair, Sassy,' Mum sighs, popping her specs on and inspecting the photo closely, 'it looks nothing like YOU either. It looks like exactly what it is. A little kid playing in her bath, grinning at her dad. So maybe you're overreacting. Just a teeny bit?'

And that's when Pip breezes in, in her little frilly nightie. I thrust the leaflet at her, pointing at the naked child, preparing myself for a shriek of horror and humiliation.

'Co-oo-oo-l!' Pip squeals happily. 'Is that me?'

'Actually, no,' Mum says. 'It's Sassy. But she doesn't want anyone to know, so we're going to say it's you. That OK, Pip, honey?'

'Co-oo-oo-l,' Pip coos again, flicking her hair. 'Do I get a fee, then? I mean, this could be my first ever modelling contract?'

That's it! I leave the kitchen. I've always suspected I'm the only sane one in this family. I will be so glad when this crazy election campaign is over. It has given my dad even more ways to ruin my life.

15

English is first thing. Thank goodness. Cos I can feel my pre-speech nerves kicking in. Like a thousand panicked butterflies hyperventilating in my tummy.

In registration I show Cordelia and Taslima one of Dad's election leaflets. Cordelia stares at the 'baby in the bath' intently for a couple of minutes. 'It looks nothing like you,' she says at last. 'Honest. For one thing that baby's totally bald. And you're totally hairy. You could quite easily pass it off as Pip.'

'I don't know,' I moan. 'I mean, *I* know it's me.'

'In that case,' Taslima says calmly, 'it's an unwanted memory and you must deal with it.'

Taslima shoves two chairs together and gets me to lie across them. 'Now,' she says in a low, hypnotic voice, 'I want you to close your eyes.'

I close my eyes and Taslima continues. 'You must visualize a small boat tied up at the edge of a river.'

'OK. I see a small brown rowing boat.'

'You must put all memories of the election leaflet into a box, and tie it up tight with string.'

'OK,' I say. 'I've done that.'

'Now put the box into the boat . . . untie the rope that's holding the boat to the shore . . . and watch the boat and the box and the unwanted memories drift off . . . and out of sight.'

My boat is just disappearing round a bend in my imaginary river when the bell rings for the end of registration. I sit up, blinking.

'How do you feel about the election leaflets now?' Taslima asks as we push our way out into the corridor.

'What election leaflets?' I smile, and Taslima nods sagely.

It takes everybody a while to settle in English. You know the way it is – when you're doing anything out of the ordinary everyone makes the most of it. In the middle of the chaos Taslima gives me my final pep talk.

'Now, you're going to be great, Sass,' she says. 'If Miss Peabody gives you the choice try to go second. It's been psychologically proven that voters will always be more sympathetic to the person who gives the last speech.'

Cordelia wraps me up in a hug and tells me she cast a special spell for me last night. 'Don't worry,' she assures me. 'It was totally environmentally friendly and involved no cruelty to animals.'

Midge Murphy's leaping about over the desks like a hyperactive chimpanzee and Sindi-Sue's new kitten-heeled shoe is flying across the room when Miss Peabody comes in. She stands in the doorway, scowling, until we all settle down. Then she calls me and Megan out to the front to present our manifestos.

'OK,' Miss Peabody says. 'Which of you would like to start?'

And I'm about to ask if it's OK if I go second when Megan says, 'I'll let Sassy go first, miss. I know how nervous she is.'

'That's very kind of you, Megan,' Miss Peabody says. And I'm about to protest that I'm not nervous at all. But if I make a fuss now it'll come across like I'm being petty. So I may as well get my bit over and done with.

I take a deep breath and go back to my desk to fetch my guitar. When I walk past Magnus he smiles up at me and my tummy melts squidgily. Fortunately no one notices.

Seconds later I'm at the front again. I do my little spiel about how the SOP Party is for our generation. We can't rely on older people to look after things, I explain. And, what's more, the older they are, the higher they've got their central heating turned up, even though the carbon dioxide emissions they produce are making global warming go faster and faster.

And then, for brain-free zones like Midge Murphy and Sindi-Sue, I explain how that means the ice caps are melting and the Siberian permafrost is turning to sludge and sea levels are rising and flooding coastal areas and new deserts are forming and more and more bits of the Earth are becoming uninhabitable so people will all start fighting over fresh water and food and invading each other's countries and we'll be lucky if we get to grow old before we die.

I've still got a few more points I'd like to make when Miss Peabody coughs politely and signals for me to wind up.

'Before I finish I'd like to sing a song I wrote myself,' I announce, picking up my guitar. As I tune the strings I'm thinking this has to be a stupid idea, but it's too late now – I can't back down.

Just before I start to play I look up, and Magnus is staring straight at me. Everyone is totally quiet, like you could hear the tiniest pin drop.

I strum a few chords, then start off.

Oh why can't people be more like dolphins?
A dolphin's face always meets you grinning
A dolphin is free – he's got no need to kill
A dolphin is happy – he swims for the thrill.

It's starting to feel OK. My voice steadies and I up the volume a bit. Then I'm racing towards the new end I've written specially for today.

> He's happy to smile while we poison his sea
> If you love our planet and want it to be
> A beautiful place where we all can live free
> It's simple, my friends. Just vote S-O-P-P!

I look up just as I finish. There's this awful moment of stunned silence. And just when I think they hated it and I've made a complete fool of myself everyone starts clapping and whooping and whistling and jumping up and down, and Miss Peabody has to slam the door hard to shock them into silence.

'Why, thank you, Sassy!' Miss Peabody beams. 'I really wasn't expecting that. You certainly made quite an impact.'

I walk back to my seat like I'm walking on air. This is the first time I've played guitar and sung a song I wrote myself in front of my classmates. And I'm so relieved they liked it.

Cordelia high-fives me as I pass.

While Megan gets organized to do her spiel Magnus scribbles something on a piece of paper, folds it and passes it along the row. Midge Murphy slips it under my desk. I glance down and my heart skips a beat. It says FOR SASSY! Cordelia gives me a quiet thumbs up, like she knows what's written inside. (Which she quite probably does.)

Ever so carefully, I open it up.

I'm still on such a high that my eyes are kind of jumpy, so I have to read it twice.

Meet you at front gate after school?
Magnus

And something inside my chest goes PING and I'm so excited I can hardly breathe!

As Megan begins her speech for the GTPWTW[19] Party I slip Magnus's note into my pocket. I want to keep it. Forever. Maybe I could get it framed. Or folded into a silver locket to wear round my neck.

Surreptitiously I tear a scrap from the corner of my exercise book and print:

OK C U there.
Sassy

I pass it back along. I am so happy!

Megan finishes her speech in about three seconds flat. So no challenge there, I'm thinking. And then she does something I am really not

[19] Give The People What They Want. Told you no one would remember it, didn't I?

expecting. She digs into her school bag, takes out all these mini choccy bars and shouts, 'VOTE FOR ME AND MAKE THE WORLD A SWEETER PLACE!'

Then she starts to throw them like she's throwing fish to the penguins at the zoo. And there's total chaos as everyone dives to catch one, and chairs and desks topple over and Miss Peabody's shouting, 'SETTLE DOWN! SETTLE DOWN!' and then everyone does because they're all stuffing their faces with chocolate and Miss Peabody wipes her brow and says, 'TIME FOR THE VOTE.' And everyone's still munching.

Me and Megan have to go out of the room while the rest of the class vote. Out in the corridor Megan holds out a mini choccy bar.

'Last one,' she says. 'I kept it for you.'

I shake my head.

'It's OK,' she smiles. 'It's not like it's poisoned.'

Just then the classroom door swings open and Miss Peabody's grey-haired head pops out.

'Time to come back in, girls!'

I breathe in deeply and cross my fingers behind my back. I know they loved the song. I mean, they went wild, didn't they? And Megan's pitch wasn't exactly serious.

'Beano, our Returning Officer, will now read out the results,' Miss Peabody announces.

Beano stands up and unfolds a sheet of paper.

'Sassy Wilde, the Save Our Planet Party . . .' He pauses for dramatic effect and I hold my breath. 'Five votes.'

I don't hear Megan's result. It's like there's an ocean roaring in my ears. Counting me and Megan, there are twenty-seven people in my class. So twenty have sold out – for a chocolate bar!

Suddenly I realize Megan's reaching out her hand. Through a blur of tears I shake it, and I'm so glad I've got my hair straight because it swings over my face and hides how upset I am.

Then the bell goes and everyone's pushing their chairs back, heaving their bags on to their shoulders, moving like a big river of molten lava out of the room.

I go to fetch my bag and my guitar. The classroom looks wrecked. Desks askew, chairs tumbled over, crumpled chocolate wrappers everywhere.

So much for my generation looking after things, I think sadly.

16

It's a good ten minutes into the next period before I recover my senses. I tug a paper hanky from my pocket and Magnus's note drifts to the floor. I pounce on it. I had almost forgotten. Just when I thought this was the worst day of my life ever!

And then a thought hits me like a hammer blow. Magnus wrote the note just after I sang. When it looked like I was going to win. Before my public humiliation and defeat.

A sick feeling grips my stomach. He's probably regretting ever writing that silly little note.

Maybe I should ask to go home early, say I've got a tummy upset or something. I mean, I don't think I could stand it if I turned up at the front gate at half three and he didn't. I've had quite enough humiliation for one day, thank you.

In Miss Cassidy's art class before lunch, Taslima and Cordelia try to calm me down. We're doing a collage thingie, which involves a lot of cutting out from old magazines.

'You're being silly,' Taslima says in her therapist's voice as she snips the heads off a row of babies. 'You weren't humiliated at all. No one was taking the election thing seriously. Honest.'

'And everyone loved your song,' Cordelia adds as she sticks some blood-red sequins along the top of her creation. 'It really was brilliant.'

'So why didn't I win, then?' I ask, terminally depressed.

'Oh that's easy,' Cordelia says, and her green eyes shine as she inks a tiny white skull and crossbones on to the black background of her collage. 'Fate was giving you a sign. You're not meant to be a politician. You're meant to be a singer.'

Just then Sindi-Sue strolls by our table. 'I loved your song, Sass.' She grins, flashing her laser-whitened teeth. 'It was brilliant, really.'

'What's this about a song?' Miss Cassidy asks. 'I feel like I've missed out on something.'

Miss Cassidy is young and really cool. She wears mad arty clothes. Big sticky-out skirts and bright pink tops with crazy buttons and flowers sewn on. Rumour has it that her anarchic dress sense infuriates Smelly Smollett, our head teacher, which, in my opinion, can only be a good thing.

'So this song?' Miss Cassidy says. 'Would you sing it for me?'

I look up in surprise.

'I'm serious,' she says. 'I'd love to hear it. Please?'

Everyone else starts going, 'Yeah, Sassy. Go for it.' So I get my guitar out, tune it – TWANG TWANG TWANG – and sing the dolphin song again.

'Well done!' Miss Cassidy says when I finish and the whole class applauds. 'You should take yourself seriously, Sassy. You're really good.'

By the time the bell rings for the end of the art lesson I feel much better.

'OK,' I say to Cordelia and Taslima. 'I'll not go home early. But I'm not going to count on Magnus turning up at half three either.'

'No sweat,' Cordelia says. 'I'll walk out with you. If he doesn't show we'll just keep walking.'

Typical! All day, while we've been stuck at our desks, it's been really lovely outside, lots of blue sky and scudding clouds. Then just before half three it starts to chuck it down. Big wet drops slap against the windows. The bell rings and Cordelia and I spill out into the damp playground.

Everyone's grumbling and tugging at their hoods or digging in their bags for umbrellas. Some of the smaller boys hoick their sweatshirts up over their heads and scuttle off like neckless aliens. I don't have a hood. And I don't have an umbrella. But I couldn't care less. All I can think about is whether or not Magnus will be there. Cordelia links arms with me and guides me through the throng of bodies.

And that's when I spot him! Over at the gate like he said. Phew! Cordelia gives my arm a squeeze and my heart starts to flutter like a distressed sparrow. Beano's with him and they're battering each other with their backpacks.

'Why can't boys just stand still and chat like normal people?' Cordelia asks.[20]

Just then Beano whacks his bag hard down on Magnus's head. It bursts open and books and pencils and all sorts of junk go scattering across the playground. *Biology 2* flies through the air. Beano dives after it and suddenly he's crouched at Cordelia's feet, looking up into her huge green eyes, like a slave staring up at a goddess.

Magnus grins at me.

Cordelia gives me a hug and turns to go. 'Bye, Sass. See you later!' she calls. Beano grabs at his scattered belongings and trots behind her like a love-struck puppy. It's almost as if she's cast a

[20] Why does Cordelia keep asking questions which cannot be answered?

spell on him – which, come to think of it, she probably has.

The playground's almost empty now.

'Hi,' says Magnus, stuffing his hands deep into his jacket pockets.

'Hi,' I say back. The rain's pattering down on my head, but I don't care.

'I've only got a few minutes. I've got swim practice,' Magnus says, looking at the ground.

'Oh!' I say, dismayed.

'I was wondering . . .' His voice trails off, as if he's not quite sure whether to continue. 'If you'd like to meet up later. Maybe about seven?'

Omigod! My tummy does its double back-flip thing and almost lands in my mouth. Has Magnus just asked me on a date?

Suddenly he looks up and stares at me, like he's scared I'm going to say no.

I'm struck dumb, brain-damaged-goldfish style. He looks SO lovely – the raindrops on his hair glistening like diamonds, his eyes the deepest blue. And he's so sweet. He obviously loved my song and didn't mind at all that I lost the vote. I mean, like Taslima said, that's what a girl setting out on a singing career needs, isn't it? Someone under-standing and supportive.

At last my voice responds. 'Sure.' I push my hair back from my face, desperately hoping I look cool.

'So where do you want to meet?' he asks.

'Where?' I echo.

Help! This is new territory for me. I've never had a date before. If it wasn't raining I might have suggested the swing park. I know some kids often meet up there later, when the little ones have gone home. But the sky's totally grey and the rain's hammering down. And I can't think of anything worse than hanging around a deserted swing park getting soaked through – even with Magnus.

'How about the caff at Paradiso's?' Magnus says suddenly.

'Cool,' I say. Then, just to prove I can manage more than one word at a time, I force myself to say something else. 'See you there, then.'

'Yeah!' Magnus smiles. Then he's gone, jogging towards the swimming block. And I'm left standing in the deserted playground, soaking wet, grinning fit to split my face in two!

17

It's only when I get home that two things hit me.

1. When you straighten naturally curly hair then stand out in the rain it frizzes up completely.
2. I have agreed to have my first ever date in a superstore I hate and completely disapprove of!

WHICH MAKES ME A SAD FRIZZY-HAIRED FREAK WHO'S SOLD OUT ON HER PRINCIPLES!

Distraught, I phone Cordelia.

'Calm down, Sass! Your hair looked absolutely fine when I left. It probably frizzed up later. Anyway,' she reasons, 'if it looked that awful he wouldn't have asked to meet up, would he?'

'But Paradiso's caff?' I wail down the phone. 'I mean, what am I going to do? I am SO against big superstores. They TOTALLY destroy the local shops and fly stuff halfway round the world causing millions of tons of greenhouse gases! And they use tons of packaging on their fruit and veg and ready meals that just add to the whole problem of waste disposal and pollution!'

There's a brief silence at the other end of the line.

'Just meet him there, then ask him back to your place,' Cordelia suggests brightly.

I think about it. That would mean he'd meet the parentals. Aaarghhh! And Pip. Double aaaargghhhh! And, for that matter, Digby, who's all but taken up residence in the campaign cupboard.

What's more, I'd have to tidy my room. You know, make sure there's nothing embarrassing lying about. Like girly things. And I don't have time for that. As it is, I'm going to have to wash my hair and straighten it again. And find some-thing to wear.

'Nah,' I groan. 'Too much hassle.'

Just then Mum comes in and I say a quick bye to Cordelia.

My heart sinks as Mum settles on the end of my bed. It's always a bad sign. It means she wants to talk SERIOUS. Or EMBARRASSING. Like do I need to move up to the next bra size. (Hmph! Chance would be a fine thing.)

Mum clears her throat and smiles. Another BAD sign.

'So what was all that about, honey?' she asks.

'Nothing,' I say hurriedly, grabbing some stuff I need for the shower.

'Well, anyway, the thing is –' she begins.

'Listen, Mum. Can we maybe talk later? I mean I'm in a bit of a rush here –'

I bang around my room, making a big show of being in a hurry, even though I'm not.

'A bit of a rush?' Mum repeats. 'Why's that?'

'I need to shower and dry my hair and straighten it and do tomorrow's homework –'

'Well, this won't take more than a couple of minutes, honey,' Mum says, picking Tiny Ted up and thoughtfully smoothing his fur. 'The thing is, I'm really sorry you didn't get to Megan's party the other night.'

Oops! A sudden pang of guilt stabs me in the gut. It's strong enough to make me think I should at least hear Mum out. I flump on to my beanbag and sigh heavily.

'I bumped into Megan's mum today,' Mum continues. 'In Paradiso's. And it sounds like the party got rather out of hand.'

'Yeah, I heard,' I lie, hoping Mum doesn't notice.

'Anyway,' Mum goes on, 'she was saying – again – how sorry she was about everything that happened, you know, when you were still in primary school. It was a very difficult time for Megan, she was saying. Things were very unsettled and unhappy at home.'

'Look, Mum. I know all this. You told me at the time. Her dad ran off with his secretary and her mum wasn't coping and was maybe even going to have to sell their house and move. I *know* all this!'

'Mrs Campbell says Megan has settled down now. She's not palling around with those older girls any more. She says that Hannah girl and her friends were just using Megan. Always borrowing her clothes and not giving them back. Getting money from her, making her run messages for them and things. Not real friends at all.'

I set my jaw and stare out of the window. Mum's idea of a couple of minutes is very different from mine. It must be something to do with getting older. Time must move slower, I suppose. I make a mental note to myself. *I will never EVER do this to my children!*

'So,' Mum continues, 'Megan's mum would dearly love you and Megan to be friends again. I was thinking, maybe you could ask her round for tea?'

My mother is certifiably insane!

'Look, Mum. I really don't have time for this. I do not want to make up with Megan –'

'Sassy, I know what she did was wrong –'

'WRONG!' I shriek, surprising even myself. 'Megan STOLE from me and CHEATED and LIED!'

Mum sighs heavily and gets up from the bed. 'Think about it, Sassy,' she says. 'I hoped when you asked to go to Megan's party you'd moved on. Bitterness breeds bitterness, honey. You need to forgive and forget.'

Minutes later I stomp along to the shower. *Why is it*, I wonder as I step under the hot spray, *that Megan constantly spoils things for me?* I'd just managed to get over this morning's humiliation, and was feeling all happy about my date with Magnus, when – PING – Megan pops up again and makes me feel all horrible and yucky.

As I dry my hair I still can't get Megan out of my head. So Mum thinks what happened at the end of Primary Seven wasn't such a big deal? Well, it was. I'd put tons of work into writing something new for this big poetry competition and then what happened? Megan's poem won.

Which would have been fine.

Except it wasn't Megan's.

It was mine.

She'd copied it out of one of my notebooks and put it into the competition under her name.

Of course, I told Miss Brown, our teacher. And

up till then I'd really, really liked Miss Brown. She'd been my favourite teacher ever.

But Miss Brown said could she see the original? And that night I turned my room upside down looking for the notebook. And I found it. But the page with the poem was ripped out.

The next day Miss Brown said she'd spoken to Megan and to Megan's mum and they'd both insisted Megan had written the poem and that it wasn't very nice of me to accuse someone who was my best friend of cheating just cos I hadn't won.

And I was so upset I burst into tears in front of the whole class and had to run out of the room, and then some of the mean girls started to follow me around and call me cry baby and tease me. Which was the last thing I needed just before I was going up to high school, which, let's face it, was scary enough on its own.

Megan has never come clean about it. She has never called to apologize or anything. Then when we started high school she hung around with older girls like Hannah and her horrible friends, and I met up with Cordelia and Taslima and it was the best thing that ever happened to me.

Anyway, at the time Mum tried to make out that I should've been big enough to help Megan through 'a rough patch'. Megan, Mum said, was just being very needy and if it was a prize I wanted then she would get me one. Which is how I got my guitar.

But, though I love my guitar, I really, honestly, don't think I can forgive Megan. Not yet.

Maybe not ever.

18

Whoopeee! The rain has stopped, my hair is straight and I, Sassy Wilde, am on my way to meet Magnus the Magnificent!

I had to lie to Mum. But it was just a little white lie. I mean it's not one that can POSSIBLY harm anyone. At thirteen a chica should be able to do some things privately without the parentals having full information. I mean, I don't ask them for every detail of where they're going, who they're going with and what they intend doing every time they step out of the house.

And if I HADN'T lied I would've been stopped at the door and the conversation would have gone something like this:

MUM: *So where are you going?*

ME: *Paradiso's caff.*

MUM: *But you hate Paradiso's! Why on earth are you going there?*

ME: *I'm meeting someone.*

MUM: *Someone? What do you mean, 'someone'? Has this someone got a name?*

ME: *Magnus.*

MUM: *Magnus? Who's Magnus?*

ME: *A boy.*

MUM: *Well, I guessed that. So where does he live?*

MUM: *How do you know him?*

MUM: *Why don't you bring him back here?*

MUM: *What are the two of you going to be doing?*

MUM: *Why can't we meet him?*

And so on. And so on. And so on.

Whereas the WHITE LIE conversation went like this:

MUM: *So where are you going?*

ME: *I'm meeting Cordelia. Up at Paradiso's.*

MUM: *That's great, cookie. Have fun!*

ME: *Byeeee!*

MUM: *Byeeee!*

With some luck I'll make it all the way to Paradiso's without it starting to rain again and my hair turning into some kind of crazy fright wig. I'm wearing my new jeans, a cool little Friends of the Fowl vest top with a silly yellow chicken on the front and my new sandals. I've straightened my hair – again – and put a smear of eyeliner round my eyes and a bit of mascara on. I thought about lip gloss, but Pip told me recently about a survey in one of Mum's magazines – which, incidentally, I don't think she should be reading! – that eighty-two per cent of men say they don't like kissing a girl with lip-gloss on. They prefer their kissing 'au naturel'.

Not, of course, that I'm planning to KISS Magnus tonight!

If we get as far as holding hands that would be just fine.

I do Taslima's calming exercise – you know, the breathe-through-your-heels trick – until at last I see Paradiso's up ahead.

The car park is pretty busy. Mums and kids everywhere. And the occasional man. But no Magnus. Then I see him. Standing by the kiddies' sit-'n'-rides. You know, the little Thomas the Tank Engine and the Spaceship.

He's wearing black shorts and a black T-shirt. Unfortunately it's got JOCKSTAR splattered across the front. Once we know each other better I'll explain to Magnus why advertising multi-nationals on your body is a BAD thing. I mean, you can't blame him for not knowing, can you? He spends most of his day underwater, training to be a swim champ.

I give him a little wave as I approach. He smiles back. My head races. What am I going to say to him? I can stand up in front of the whole class – or the whole school, for that matter – and blast forth on the need to cut carbon emissions and recycle your old socks, but I lose the ability to string two words together when I'm anywhere near Magnus.

Suddenly I'm by his side. The electronic doors glide soundlessly open and we're walking through. Together. He's saying something, but it all jumbles in my head so I just smile and laugh and hope he's not just told me his gran's died or his cat got run over.

And then we're in the queue in the caff and Magnus has taken a tray and he's filling a paper cup with Fizzipop and asking me what I'd like. But my head's thinking Fizzipop's another multi-national company with really dodgy practices stealing the water supplies in some Third World countries, and it's full of chemicals and things that'll make me hyper, and then I hear myself saying, 'Fizzipop's great, thanks,' and he's filling another paper cup and it all froths up and spills over the top and over his hand and he's laughing and I try to tug a couple of napkins from the dispenser to help mop it up when the whole dispenser splits open and a thousand napkins flutter everywhere.

Five minutes later Magnus has tidied up the napkins, and paid, and carried the Fizzipops safely back to a table. I'm so relieved to be sitting down. I try to breathe through my heels without Magnus seeing. I SO need to get a grip.

Magnus is chatting away. He did the Scottish

qualifying time at the swim thing he went to in Edinburgh, so there's a chance he'll be in the national youth team! Thank goodness he's doing the talking. My heartbeat starts to slow. There. I even manage to take a sip of my drink without it choking me and spurting down my nose. Magnus has given me two straws. I smile at him as I suck. He sucks from his Fizzipop and smiles back. It is SO romantic. My backbone goes all tingly and turns to jelly.

'You were brilliant in the mock election,' he says.

At last I find my voice. 'Thanks. But I didn't win.'

'But your song was really good.'

I smile at him again.

'I didn't know you could play guitar and sing. It was cool.'

That's when I realize I am a sucker for flattery! Like Brewster with his dog biscuits, I wait patiently to be fed more.

'And you look great with your hair straight. I saw you at Megan's. You should wear a dress more often. It really suits you.'

At last I relax, and soon we're talking quite naturally. About school, and Mr Hemphead's stick insects, which he breeds in big glass tanks all round his room. And Magnus says he went in to see Mr Hemphead one lunchtime and

127

Mr Hemphead had a huge stick insect on his desk and was sharing his jalapeño sandwich with it, and talking to it – like it was a real person. And I suddenly realize that Mr Hemphead actually LOOKS like a stick insect and we both have a fit of the giggles.

Then we start to talk about Miss Peabody and how ancient and funny she is.

'Have you ever noticed,' Magnus asks, 'she's always got these huge knitting needles sticking out of her bag?'

'I know!' I laugh. 'And she's been knitting the same thing forever. That horrible orange wool! I can't believe she's ever going to wear it.'

And that's when I see him. Over by the Fair Trade bananas. A huge green rosette in his lapel, a small crowd of photographers and reporters buzzing round him.

MY DAD!!!

Magnus follows my gaze. 'Somebody you know?' he asks.

And I'm about to say, 'No, not really,' and suggest to Magnus we should maybe go, NOW, when Digby spots me. Immediately he whooshes over, grinning from ear to ear.

'Hey! Sassy! This is great!' he exclaims. 'Perfect, in fact!'

My heart sinks and my brain whirrs into overdrive. Mum thinks I'm with Cordelia. Magnus looks nothing like Cordelia. Oh no! If Dad finds out I fibbed I'll never get my demo disc. I have learned through bitter experience that the atrophying[21] parental brain just cannot grasp the difference between a teensy white fib and a **HUGE GREAT WHOPPING LIE**.

'Now, who's your friend?' Digby asks, stretching a hand out to Magnus.

'Magnus,' I mutter. 'This is Digby.'

'Tell you what, Magnus,' Digby says as he shakes his hand vigorously. 'I'd just like to borrow Sassy for a few moments. Then you can have her back.'

Magnus looks confused. And I'm confused too. Since when did I become an object to be lent or borrowed? But Digby has already got me by the arm and he's dragging me towards the Special Offers.

'Your father's doing a photo call,' he whispers as he whisks me along. 'You know, part of the election campaign. *Dad Does Weekly Shop*. That kind of thing. We've got the local press here. So if you could just be in for a couple of dad-and-daughter shots, that would be perfect!'

---

[21] A word Taslima is very fond of. Got something to do with shrinking. Think of a grape turning into a raisin, Taslima says. Or a plum turning into a prune. *Our* brains are plums. Our parentals' brains are prunes.

Dad looks momentarily startled as Digby propels me towards him.

'But –' I start to protest.

Too late.

Like an experienced politician, Dad covers his surprise, slings his arm around me and grins at the cameras. He even kisses the top of my head. YEEEUCK!

Through a blur of flashing lights I see Magnus – staring. Oh no! How am I going to look him in the eye after this? I am SO embarrassed.

'Smile, Sassy!' Digby mouths, towering above the heads of the photographers.

'Can we have one by the meat counter?' one of the photographers calls, and everyone files off.

By the meat counter? THE MUTILATED, DEAD ANIMAL COUNTER? I don't think so. This far and no further! One of the reporters grabs Dad to ask his views on the comparative benefits of genetically modified runner beans. I would love to answer him, but instead take my chance and escape down the Pickles and Jams aisle.

But where's Magnus? I have to double back to find him. And guess what? He's only hanging on Dad's every word, excited, his face shining! Like genetically modified runner beans were all he'd been waiting for to make his life complete.

'Wow, Sassy! You never said your dad was famous!' he exclaims.

'He's not,' I hiss. 'And I'm going. Are you coming?'

I half expect him to say no. I mean, he looks more in love with my dad than with me!

'Sure,' Magnus says meekly, and follows in my wake as I tank towards the exit.

After we leave the supermarket Magnus walks me to the end of my road. He says it's great I got into the photo with my dad. He says he doesn't think it's embarrassing at all. And he says he's going to get the local newspaper when it comes out, and he's going to cut the picture out and get me to sign it in case I'm famous one day and he'll be able to sell it for lots of money. Except, he says, he won't sell it, cos he'll want to keep it. And when he says that he looks into my eyes, like he's really kinda crazy about me, and I start to feel all squidgy inside again.

Which makes me all nervous so I start rabbiting on about the deal I did with Dad for the demo disc and what a great opportunity it is and how I really want to write and play my own songs – when who comes hurtling towards us, weaving crazily on a skateboard, but Megan's stepbro, Twig.

Of course, I try to ignore him. But just as he passes he flicks the board up, catches it and leaps on to the pavement, yelling, 'Hiya!' like he's a mate. 'I was just coming to see you. There's some-thing I need to talk to you about.' He fires a look at Magnus. 'In private.'

Magnus bristles and puts his arm round me!

My heart almost stops, then starts to race. And I'm sure I can feel Magnus pulling himself up tall, just like Brewster used to if any other dogs came sniffing around his lovely black lady lab.[22]

A bit of me likes it. A bit hates it. Like there's these two tiny versions of me in a boxing ring inside my head. In the pink corner, the new Sassy, with her straight hair and her teensy glam dress, is checking her lip gloss in a mirror. And in the green corner, the old Sassy, her hair crazily curly, in jeans and a vest top, not wanting any guy to have any rights over her, or any say over what she does and who she sees, flexes her muscles and limbers up.

'Whatever,' I say to Twig. 'But right now's not a good time.'

At last he clicks he's not wanted and leaps back on his board.

'See ya soon!' he says, and speeds off.

'So who's he?' Magnus asks, dropping his arm from my shoulder.

'Twig,' I mutter, expecting that to be the end

[22] Who sadly passed away a few months ago. Poor Brewster. He's still in mourning.

of the matter. Some hope! From there to the end of the road Magnus doesn't shut up about Twig. *What's his real name? What school does he go to? How do you know him?*

I don't know the answers to half his questions – and, to be perfectly honest, I don't want to answer the other half. I mean, no way am I going to tell him about Twig finding me slumped in a puddle of tears on the pavement on Friday night.

So in the end I say, 'Look, can we change the subject? He's just this boy. I really don't want to talk about him.'

And can you believe it? Magnus only goes all moody on me.

'Spit on a stick!' I exclaim, exasperated. 'If you want to know about Twig go ask Megan. He's HER new stepbro. He's got nothing to do with me!'

'Honest?'

'Honest.'

We stop at the end of my road cos I'm not letting Magnus near any of my family again – not for a long time – when Brewster comes ambling along, sniffing the air, to meet us.

'Here, boy! Over here!' I call softly. I think maybe Magnus is a bit scared of dogs, cos he doesn't immediately start tickling Brewster's ears or doing the kind of things doggy people do.

Then, before I can stop him, Brewster starts sniffing Magnus's shorts! It's so embarrassing. Honestly, I don't know where to look. I thought Brewster was the one member of the family I could trust. I grab his collar and drag him off and start blabbering on about how Brewster is blind and how his lady love died and he's really not been the same since. As if that in some way excuses his anti-social behaviour!

But at least it gets us both laughing again and we climb up on to the wall that borders the woods so Brewster can't make any more unseemly advances. Then we chat for a while and Magnus asks if maybe I'll write a song for him sometime. I blush and don't let on I already have.

When it's time for him to go, we don't kiss or anything. Thank goodness! I need some advice or training first. Maybe the Girl Guides could introduce the Snogging Badge. They could ask the Boy Scouts to volunteer as guinea pigs. It would be a whole lot more useful than the Brownie Skills Badge I got for sewing on a button, tying a knot, washing my hands, reading a map and addressing an envelope. And a whole lot more fun.

Or maybe on their thirteenth birthday every new teen could get a kissing guide and video. Something like *Snogging for Idiots* might be a good start.

Anyway, just before he leaves, Magnus says, 'So are you my girlfriend now?'

And I say, 'Yes.'

And he says, 'See you tomorrow!'

Then he goes jogging up the road. And just as he disappears round the corner, he leaps up and punches the air, like he's really happy.

Which I am too.

I think.

19

Breakfast this morning was somewhat fraught.

First I had to skilfully evade Dad's THREE THOUSAND AND ONE QUESTIONS I MUST ASK ABOUT THIS BOY MAGNUS, by screaming at him to butt out of my life and get on with his silly election campaign.

Then guess what? He only INSISTED I APOLOGIZE to MUM for FIBBING about who I was meeting last night. Luckily, though, she's just finished a chapter in her book called 'Secrecy and the Teenage Psyche'. 'No need to overreact,' she pointed out calmly. 'Sassy is actually behaving normally.' And Dad was so astonished he burned the toast.

Finally I had to tell Pip IN NO UNCERTAIN TERMS I will NOT be bringing Magnus home to meet her for quite some time. If ever.

As a result I am now going to be late for school. Which is why I hurtle out of the house at breakneck speed and trip over Twig, who's sitting – uninvited – on my front doorstep.

'Do you mind?' I squeak, rubbing my shin, which has collided painfully with his skull. 'What exactly are you doing?'

Twig squints up at me through his tousle of hair. Brewster's lying across his lap, almost purring with pleasure. I shoo Brewster away and he lopes mournfully off. Instantly I feel bad. It's Twig I want to be horrible to, not Brewster.

'I'm waiting for you,' Twig says, massaging the back of his head as he gets to his feet.

'You shouldn't have bothered,' I say loftily. 'Some people go to school, you know.' And I stride off down the path.

Twig follows me.

'Hold on! Please?' He jumps the fence and plants himself in front of the gate.

I make a big play of looking at my watch and sighing heavily. Biology's first thing and I'm hoping to get paired up with Magnus.

'Please move out of my way,' I say firmly. Twig isn't much bigger than me. And slight. If I push hard enough I can easily barge past him. And I will if I have to.

'Your name's Sassy, isn't it?'

I roll my eyes.

'Well, I'm Twig.'

'I know,' I mutter, 'you told me already.' I'm too late for registration now, so there's no point in rushing. If I'm lucky I'll be able to slip straight into biology without Smollett seeing me.

'There's something I want to show you,' he blurts.

'Is that a chat-up line?' I tease.

'No, there really is something I want to show you!' His cheeks go pink. 'In the woods.'

'You're making it worse,' I smile.

'Seriously, Sassy, you were wearing a Friends of the Fowl T-shirt last night and you sang that song about dolphins and things, so –'

'So?'

'So I thought you might care –'

'Care about what?' I ask, curious now.

'About Bluebell Wood.'

'Of course I care about Bluebell Wood! In fact, I care about all woods. Everywhere.'

Twig brightens. 'Look, this will only take a couple of minutes. Just come with me. See for yourself. It's important.'

I glance at my watch. If I go to school without finding out what he's so worked up about it'll bug me all day. And if I'm quick I should still be able to make the start of biology.

'OK,' I say, following him along the road to the wood. 'But this had better be good.'

When we reach the first trees Twig leads the way down the main path. After a few hundred metres he cuts off through the bushes.

I pick my way along behind him, and I'm just thinking maybe this is all a big wind-up – after all, Megan did say he was a bit weird – when Twig turns and signals to me to keep down.

And that's when I see him. A man in a suit, with an orange hard hat on, like they wear on building sites. He moves between the trees, stopping every so often to make notes on a clipboard.

Twig looks at me.

'What's he doing?' I whisper.

'That's what I want to find out. He was here yesterday too. Up at the other end of the woods.'

'So maybe he's a tree surgeon?'

'Tree surgeons don't wear suits,' Twig whispers. 'And he had one of those measuring camera things on a tripod with him yesterday. I checked his car out too. The back seat's covered with plans. Like they're planning to build something here –'

'But they can't!' I gasp.

Too loud.

The man spins round and spots us. Twig crouches lower. But I don't. I stand up as if there's nothing at all odd about being discovered in the bushes.

The man eyes me for a moment. 'Shouldn't you be in school, kid?' he says, frowning.

'Shouldn't you be in an office?' I smile as I wipe some cobwebs from my shoulder.

He sighs heavily. 'Look. I've got work to do. Why don't you just run along?' He turns his back and makes another note on his clipboard.

'What kind of work?' I ask, struggling out of the bushes and moving towards him.

'None of your business.' He holds the clipboard close to his chest.

'No, no! It is my business!' I insist, swinging my backpack off and unzipping it.

The man rolls his eyes and takes his mobile out. 'Look, kid. Get lost – NOW – or I'll call your headmaster.' He eyes my uniform. 'Strathcarron High? That'll be Mr Smollett. I'll just call him, let him know you're skipping class . . .'

'Don't be silly!' I giggle. 'Mr Smollett knows I'm here. In fact, my whole class is here. It's part of our environmental studies project.' I pull a notebook and pencil from my bag. 'All about Bluebell Wood. So maybe I could just do a short interview with you?'

I sit down on a boulder, open the notebook and lick the top of my pencil like they do in old police movies. 'So if you'd like to tell me your name, and what you're doing here?' I ask, as authoritatively as possible.

He stares down at me. 'Look, I'm counting the trees. That's all you need to know.'

'Counting trees . . .' I repeat, writing it down. 'So why are you counting the trees?'

He sighs heavily. 'I really don't have time for this.'

'But it would be such a great help for our project! And I'm so glad I found you before any of the others. It's like getting a scoop, isn't it? And my teacher will be really pleased.'

Just then there's a loud CRACK from the bushes. I guess it's Twig. 'That'll be my friend, Twig!' I say. The man scowls at me.

'Honestly, it is his name!' I smile. 'He's the photographer on the project. But he's very shy. He's probably taking photos of us right now.'

'Look, I don't want my photo taken,' the man says, holding his clipboard up in front of his face.

'Why not?' I ask sweetly.

Just then the man's mobile rings and he stomps off through the trees. 'I can't talk right now,' I hear him muttering. 'The whole place is crawling with school kids. I'm coming back to the office.'

'Thank you ever so much for your help!' I call cheerily after him. 'We're going to be here all day!'

'Wow!' says Twig, emerging from the under-growth, wide-eyed as a bush baby. 'That was amazing! Whatever he's up to, you've scared him off. For today at least.'

I tuck my notebook back in my rucksack, trying to make out it was no big deal, but my tummy feels a bit tight and sick.

'So what do you think he's up to?' I ask quietly. 'I mean, I can't think it's anything good, or he would have just told me, wouldn't he?'

Twig leans against the trunk of a huge old beech tree and looks up through the green canopy of leaves. Beyond them the sky's a beautiful blue.

'I think they're going to build something here,' he says. 'Houses or shops or something.'

'But they'd need to get, what do you call it . . . planning permission . . . wouldn't they?'

Twig shrugs. 'They're supposed to. But once the trees are chopped down, you can't put them back up again, can you? So some developers take their chance. Go ahead without it.'

I look around the woods. A squirrel runs up the trunk of one of the trees. Birds dart through the branches. The sound of birdsong fills the air. I love it here. It's the only place in Strathcarron where you feel you're away from all the roads and buildings and concrete. The only place where you can feel truly alive. I breathe in deeply. The air is fresh and sweet. Like you can smell the greenness, almost taste it on your tongue.

'Have you told anyone else about this?' I ask.

'I only moved here a couple of weeks ago.'

Twig smiles. 'So I don't know anyone. Except Megan, of course. But what's the point in telling her? If they want to build more shops here she'll probably turn up to cheer them on.'

'She wasn't always like that,' I say, surprising myself, cos it's almost like I'm defending her. 'We were best buds all through primary. But she changed, you know, when her parents split up.'

'Yeah, that's a tough call,' he says quietly. 'It kinda knocks you sideways for a bit.'

We both sit quiet for a few minutes.

'I don't want them to change this place,' I say as a pale yellow butterfly flutters by. 'But I don't see what I can do about it.'

'But look what you've done already!' Twig says, suddenly animated. 'You're a true eco-warrior! The way you scared that guy off. I could never have been as clever as that. *And* you were so funny!'

I smile at Twig. It's sweet that he thinks I'm clever. And funny.

'But I don't see what else I can do,' I say.

'We need to let people know Bluebell Wood is under threat. Start a campaign. I'm new here. No one knows me. But you've got friends,' he says. 'Contacts.'

'No,' I say suddenly, remembering the dire warnings Dad gave me about the Paradiso's Panties Incident and the promise I made not to get into any trouble. 'I can't get involved.'

Twig looks at me like I've lost the plot. 'But why not?'

'Because I made a promise to my dad. He's standing for election and –'

'Your dad's standing for election?' Twig exclaims, so excited he's almost dancing. 'That's perfect. Don't you see? He can make it an election issue. Get media coverage! That's brilliant!'

Of course! Why hadn't I thought of that? If they're planning to destroy our woods without us knowing then that's a hot local issue.

This could be EXACTLY what Dad's campaign needs!

20

Determined to speak to Dad as soon as he gets home tonight, I leave Twig in the woods and dash off towards the school.

But I don't go in by the gate. From bitter experience I know Smelly Smollett will be lurking there, his bald pate glinting in the sun, eager to scoop up any latecomers and march them off to his office for some mindless torture.

Instead I climb the back wall, sprint across the playing fields and skip in the side door the seniors always jam open so their sleepy mates can straggle in late.

I straighten my uniform, then walk casually along the corridor, hoping against hope I don't bump into any teachers. I'm almost at the door of Mr Hemphead's biology room – where Magnus will (I hope) be pining for me – when Mr Lovelace, Magnus's swim coach and principal PE teacher, appears at the far end of the corridor.

There's something about Mr Lovelace that gives me the heebie-jeebies.

It might be the fact that he always wears tiny red shorts three sizes too small. Or the way he prowls the corridors with a mean and hungry glint in his eye.

'You! Girl!' he bellows and I stop in my tracks.

He stands, hands on hips, rising up and down on the balls of his feet as he waits for me to walk the long lonely length of the corridor towards him.

'What's your name?' he barks when at last I'm standing in front of him.

And I don't know why. I honestly don't. But suddenly I hear myself saying, 'Megan, sir. Megan Campbell.'

He nods slowly. 'Why are you not in class, Megan?'

Oh no! What am I going to say? 'I've been at the dentist's, sir.' I flash my teeth at him. 'Just got my train tracks off.'

Mr Lovelace squints at me like he's trying to decide whether or not to believe me. And, yes, it's true! I cannot deny it! And I will forever feel ashamed for doing it. But I do that fluttery thing with my eyes that Pip always does when she wants to come over all sugary-seductively sweet.

His expression softens. 'Well, run along, Megan,' he says. 'Don't keep Mr Hemphill waiting.'

The bell for the end of first period rings just as, almost collapsing under the weight of the guilt of the lie I've just told, I reach the biology room door.

Moments later Taslima and Cordelia come out and link arms with me. Magnus passes, heading in the opposite direction. He gives me a big wave. Megan clocks him and I swear she looks so furious that her perfectly straight hair frizzles.

'You're OK,' Taslima laughs as we wander into maths. 'Mr Hemphead took the register and when he called your name Cordelia had this hunch you were just late, so she did this great impersonation of you shouting, "HERE, MR HEMPHEAD, SIR."'

'And,' says Cordelia, adjusting her scarlet hair ribbons, 'I think he must have that senile dimension thing, cos ALL PERIOD he didn't even notice you weren't there.'

Great! That's even better than I could have hoped for. But even if I'd got detention for being late it would have been worth it. When it comes to doing the right thing suffering an hour's detention is nothing. Ask Nelson Mandela. Stuck in prison on Robben Island for twenty-seven years to protest against apartheid in South Africa. That's

TWICE as long as I've been alive – but he survived, because he knew deep down his cause was just.

I don't see Magnus again till last period in English. He grins at me when he comes into the room and heads straight for my desk.

'I've got swim practice after school,' he says. 'Got more time trials coming up. Maybe I could text you later?'

'Do you want my number, then?' I ask.

'Sure,' he says, and sticks out his hand. 'Write it there.'

Shakily I print the number on to the back of Magnus's hand. Just as Megan arrives. She fires Magnus a filthy look, then tosses her long blonde hair like she couldn't care less.

I smile sweetly at her as Magnus goes to his seat. Deep inside I'm going, *Wey-hey! One to Sassy. Nil to Megan!*

As Miss Peabody launches into a passionate explanation of romantic love in *Romeo and Juliet* I sit deep in troubled thought. Who would have imagined that a pacifist and animal-rights campaigner like me could get so much pleasure from a fellow human being's suffering?

I make a mental note to speak to Taslima. Maybe this is how Vlad the Impaler first got a taste for inflicting pain. Maybe he had a childhood friend who'd done him a dreadful wrong and then one day he made them suffer and discovered he quite liked it. Next thing he was chopping people's heads off and sticking them up on stakes all round the city walls.

Who knows, a well-timed spot of therapy in his teenage years from a good friend might have stopped him. Before it was all too late.

21

As soon as Dad gets home I corner him and Digby in the campaign cupboard. They listen carefully while I tell them about Bluebell Wood and the man with the clipboard.

'So what you're saying, Sassy, is that you bunked off school this morning,' Dad says sternly.

I stare at him in disbelief. 'That's hardly the point, is it?' I exclaim.

'Oh yes it is!' Dad fumes. 'I ask you to behave like a model daughter for three weeks. You promise you will. And next thing you're skipping off school, going into the woods – with some boy you don't even know!'

'Let's just cool it here,' Digby says bravely. 'Sassy knows she should have been at school on time. Right, Sassy?'

I nod.

'So it won't happen again, will it, Sassy?'

Tight-lipped, I nod again. I daren't open my mouth or, I swear, I will explode all over my father, messier than a boiled egg in a microwave, and my demo disc will be gone forever. Which would be so sad, cos I've only one more week left to behave.

Dad sighs. 'So where's this going, Digby?'

'Sassy has brought us some information. We should look into it. I've got a mate in the planning department. I'll get on to him first thing. We'll take it from there. But what mustn't happen, Sassy,' he fixes me with a steely stare, 'is you going off on some wild campaign with only half the information. You must leave this to the adults. Let us deal with it.'

'That's fine by me,' I snap, 'because, to be perfectly honest, I've got more important things to be doing with my time.'

'Ooooh!' squeals Pip from the living room. 'Like snoggy-wogging your new boyfriends!' And then she makes all these disgusting lip-smacking sounds.

Honestly! That child needs putting into some correctional facility before it's too late. I mean, when I was nine I was more interested in baby seals than boys.

And what does she mean, boyfriends?! Plural?!

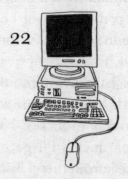

22

At lunchtime the following day Magnus grabs five minutes to share a blueberry muffin with me. I was a bit disappointed he didn't text last night – not that I was sitting by my mobile waiting or anything. I mean, my guitar practice schedule keeps me pretty busy too.

Magnus explains between mouthfuls of muffin that he's going off for the next two days to some swim training camp for mega-talented under-sixteens. When he comes back, he suggests, smiling kinda shyly, maybe we could meet up at Paradiso's caff again.

This time I refuse, on account, I explain, of not wanting to support a large multinational supermarket chain. Careful not to spray him with half-chewed muffin crumbs, I tell him how large companies keep workers' wages down, rip off local farmers and contribute to global warming by flying all sorts of goods halfway round the world.

I don't know if they're driving him too hard

on the training front, but his eyes kinda glaze over before I finish.

'I'm gonna be late for swim practice,' he says, looking at his watch. 'I need to go.'

But my little speech must have lit some passion deep inside him, cos before he speeds off he pulls me close and – yes!yes!yes! – kisses me on the cheek!

I almost choke on a half-swallowed lump of muffin, then something inside my tummy goes WHOOSH right up through me. Like a massive electric charge. And every organ in my body pings awake and every nerve ending totally zings!

I light up like I'm wired to the national grid.

I find Cordelia and Taslima sitting on the fire-exit doorstep. Cordelia's busy reading Taslima's palm, but stops as soon as she sees me.

'Karumba!' Cordelia says, shading her eyes, like I'm mega-floodlight-bright. 'You look like you're glowing!'

And I am! I continue glowing all the way through maths and French. We're in IT now, and I'm still glowing. In fact I'm giving off such an electric charge my computer's getting the jitters. This weird black graph has come up on the screen, with a bright green line peaking and dipping constantly. I press Escape and another graph pops up. Taslima leans over and presses Control+Alt+Delete, but nothing helps. Even more graphs pop up. Then the computer starts to whirr, like it's having a panic attack.

'Mrs Smith!' Taslima calls, waving her pink pencil in the air. 'There's something wrong with Sassy's computer. I think it's having a nervous breakdown.'

'Not the only one,' Mrs Smith mutters, though I don't think she meant us to hear. Sighing heavily she tucks her romantic novel, *Moonlight Becomes Her*, into the filing cabinet and comes over.

'What have you done, Sassy?' Mrs Smith asks wearily.

'Nothing, miss. Honest,' I plead.

'She's in love,' Taslima says.

Mrs Smith presses a few keys. More bright graphs appear. The toolbar at the bottom of the screen fills up with hundreds of little baby ones, all marching along.

'In love, eh? So who's the lucky fellow?' Mrs Smith asks, like she finds that more interesting than my malfunctioning computer. I hesitate. This is embarrassing. It's one thing BEING in love. Quite another sharing it with the WORLD.

'With Magnus,' Taslima whispers.

Mrs Smith's eyes widen. 'Magnus Menzies, the swim champ?'

Taslima nods.

'Nice one, Sassy.' Mrs Smith winks at me. 'He's gorgeous!'

Taslima stifles a squeal of laughter. My computer whines like a dying cat and the screen goes totally black. And me? I continue glowing.

I glow all the way home. I'm still glowing when Dad and Digby come in at six. But I haven't forgotten about Bluebell Wood. An eco-warrior-babe has to find a happy medium between her love life and her responsibilities to the planet.

'So?' I ask them right away. 'What have you found out?'

They exchange a shifty look.

And why?

Only because they have done nothing! Zilch. A big fat zero.

Digby, suitably blushing, explains how his mate is off sick. He's waiting for him to come back. Then he'll be straight on to it.

As if someone has just thrown my mains switch, I stop glowing.

'W-what you have to understand,' Digby stammers, 'is these things have to be handled delicately. They take time.'

This proves my whole theory about who should be in charge of running the world. As I have always suspected, adults are not to be trusted. Put simply: they just don't care enough.

23

After tea I phone Cordelia and tell her the whole sorry saga. 'I don't think they're going to do anything to help,' I sigh.

'Well, maybe we should go down to the woods. See if anything else has happened. I mean, if we find trees chopped down that'll force your dad and Digby to get their sorry little butts into gear, won't it?' Cordelia says.

Half an hour later I meet her at the main path into the woods. She's wearing the sweetest red frilled dress with black stripy tights and lacy fingerless gloves.

I take her the same way Twig took me. We stop in the clearing where we saw the man in the suit. A fluffy red squirrel runs up a tree and leaps delicately from branch to branch.

'This is pointless,' I mutter, sitting down on a mossy tree stump. 'Maybe the guy *was* just counting the trees or something.'

'Shhh!' Cordelia says, spreading her fingers wide.

In the distance a woodpecker taps furiously. Close by, some bigger birds, wood pigeons maybe, flutter up from the high branches, the whirring of their wings fading as they fly off.

Cordelia stretches her arms out and closes her eyes. 'I can feel something,' she whispers, swaying gently backwards and forwards. 'Yes! The trees are afraid. I feel them quivering. They feel threatened.'

She opens her eyes and slowly walks deeper into the wood, like she's in a trance. Suddenly she stops and shouts, 'Sassy! I knew it! Come and see this!'

She's standing by a huge old beech tree, her hand against its smooth bark. At first I can't see what she's so excited about. Then she lifts her hand and reveals a small splash of luminous green paint.

She moves to another tree and shouts me over. It has the luminous green mark too. Then another, and another, and another.

'What does it all mean?' Cordelia asks, eyes huge.

'It means they're marked for chopping down. That's what it means,' a voice calls from somewhere above us.

Startled, we look up into the thick green foliage. It's Twig!

'Have you been following us?!' I shriek, outraged.

'No way!' he says as he swings himself down from his perch. 'I was here first. Anyway, has your dad found out what's going on?'

'Nope,' I admit. 'That's why we're here. Checking things out.'

'There's a bad presence here. Something evil,' Cordelia whispers. 'I'm telling you. The trees feel threatened. I can feel them quivering.'

Twig widens his eyes at me, a smile playing at the corners of his mouth.

'Cordelia's psychic,' I explain. 'Her mum's a witch.'

'Course she is.' Twig nods.

Suddenly, as if possessed, Cordelia takes off again. She scoots through the bushes then rummages in the depths of a clump of ferns.

'Looks like someone's been littering!' she exclaims as she pulls out an aerosol can and gives it a shake. 'And it's not even empty!'

'You know what bugs me?' Twig says as we inspect the can. 'If we spray-paint it's called vandalism, but when grown-ups do it they call it work.'

'So what do we do now?' I ask.

'People really need to know these woods are under threat,' Twig says, tucking the can into a deep pocket of his baggy jeans. 'If not, we'll come out one morning and they'll be gone. All chopped down. And there'll be houses or factories or a road or something here instead.'

'You're right,' I say. 'Dad's out at a public meeting tonight. Trying to save a car factory – can you believe it? As soon as he gets back I'll talk to him again. He's GOT to listen this time.'

When Dad gets in just after nine I start pressing my case. He looks at me like he's no idea what I'm talking about.

'Bluebell Wood?' he repeats, gormlessly.

I roll my eyes in despair. Since my father started this whole going-into-politics caper he's become even more of an idiot than he was before.

'Right now we're chock-a-block with other things, Sassy. Your dad's got to get out and on to the doorsteps,' Digby says, marking more engagements on the election calendar he's pinned to the wall. 'As it is, he's got two public debates tomorrow about this threatened car-factory closure. And a Bonny Baby Competition. But we will get round to it, Sassy. I promise.'

I am not impressed. 'I don't think you should be campaigning to save a car factory anyway. I mean, the last thing we need is more cars!'

'It's not just about cars, Sassy. It's about jobs. And votes. The car factory is a big local employer.

Now kindly get out of my study and let us get on with things!' Dad says firmly.

To be perfectly honest I hope my dad doesn't get elected. He's just going to be like every other politician. Scared to do the right thing in case it loses him a few votes.

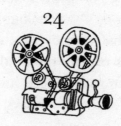

24

The next day a rumour starts spreading around the school, virulent as bird flu in a chicken coop. It goes like this:

Midge Murphy, our class idiot, says he heard from his brother, who heard from his friend who heard from this guy whose sister was going out with a fella who works in our flea-pit cinema, that the council is going to knock down the old cinema and replace it with a state-of-the-art new one. And they're going to build a new swimming pool too.

Even Miss Peabody has heard. 'It would be a wonderful thing for the town,' she says. 'It's high time there were more places for young people. It's very unhealthy having you all hanging about on the streets, being hoodies and doing that slappy-happy thing. It's not safe for a woman to go out on her own.'

'So that's what she carries those for,' Taslima whispers, nodding at the knitting needles sticking out from Miss Peabody's bag. 'They're poison-tipped weapons. For self-defence purposes.'

In art everyone's still talking about the new cinema, but Miss Cassidy says we shouldn't get too excited. It's exactly the kind of thing politicians come out with before an election to get people to vote for them, she says, but once they're elected nothing happens.

As soon as I get home I head straight for my room. There's only one more week until the election. One more week till I get the chance to cut my demo disc. All I have to do is lie low and not do anything to upset Dad. At the end of class Miss Cassidy asked me to stay behind. She gave me contact numbers for a couple of recording studios in Glasgow, and offered to help set it up for me if I want.

As I strum my guitar a new song starts to form in my head. A line comes to me. I pick up a kind of rhythm from it and the next line floats in, like waves washing gently up on the shore, one after the other.

> Don't put that axe to my throat
> Don't spray toxic fumes in my face

I'm just noting the first lines down in my notebook when my door slams open and Pip bursts in.

'Isn't it great?' Pip says, flopping on to my beanbag and grinning at me.

'Great?' I echo, absent-mindedly. 'What?'

'Oh, Sassy!' Pip rolls her eyes and flaps her tiny painted fingernails. 'You are so weird. What planet are you on? The new cinema thingie, of course!'

'It's just a rumour, Pip. You'll learn. Every so often there's a rumour about something fantastic that's going to happen in Strathcarron. It never does!'

Pip gets to her feet. 'You are such a misery, Sasperilla Wilde! Why can't you just enjoy things like other people?' She stomps across the room and turns just as she's going out of the door. 'When I grow up, I am *not* going to turn into a misery guts like you!'

'**DON'T EVER CALL ME SASPERILLA!**' I yell after her. '**OR YOU'LL NEVER GET THE CHANCE TO GROW UP!**'

I slam my room door shut and start to play guitar really loud. Whenever Pip wants to wind me up she calls me Sasperilla. Which is the name my completely idiotic parents put on my birth certificate, not thinking of the terrible psychological damage it would do. Imagine calling a child after some awful American pop soda! Thankfully, Mum's post-natal hormones had settled down by the time I was starting school, and she registered me as Sassy,[23] which is what I've always been called. So no one outside of the

---

[23] Mum's a bit dyslexic. I think she just chickened out of trying to spell Sasperilla.

Wilde household knows my dark secret. A secret I intend taking with me to the grave.

STRUMSTRUMSTRUMPITYSTRUM!

I'm doing a kind of mad punk thing, leaping around the room, swinging my hair, making such a racket I don't hear my mobile ping. Fortunately it lights up too.

I pounce on it like a cat on a gerbil.

A new text message. From Magnus! I flop back on to my bed and hold the mobile above my head. Wabby-dabby-doo! He's back! And he wants to meet up. Tonight. There's a brilliant film on at the cinema. Do I want to go?

Of course I want to go! But I've got no credit on my mobile, so I clatter downstairs two at a time and almost flatten Brewster, who has the unfortunate habit of lying at the bottom. Startled, he starts banging into the furniture and barking – just as the grandfather clock starts chiming.

'Will you stop that infernal racket!' Pip screams from the top of the stairs. 'I am trying to DO MY HOMEWORK!!!'

I run into the kitchen where Mum and Dad and Digby are poring over piles of musty old papers all tied up with pink ribbons. Weird or what?

'Can I go to the cinema tonight?' I ask quickly, fingers and legs crossed, touching wood and sending up a silent prayer to any god-like person who might be tuning in.

'Shhhhh . . .' Dad says. 'This is complicated.'

Mum looks up. 'Who with?' she mutters.

'Magnus,' I say quickly. 'You know, the NICE boy Dad met in Paradiso's.'

'OK, honey,' Mum mumbles, as she goes back to flicking through the pile of yellowed papers she's holding. 'But straight home after.'

'Thanks, Mum!' I grin. I run back into the hall and Brewster starts barking again. I shush him as I grab the phone. Hands shaking, I dial quickly. It rings. And rings. And rings. At last Magnus answers.

'Hi. It's me,' I say, trying to sound cool. 'Just got your message.'

'So . . . do you want . . . you know . . . to go?' he mumbles.

'Sure. What time?'

'Half six,' he says more brightly. 'I can meet you at the end of your road if you want. We can walk up together.'

'Brilliant,' I say.

Because – WABBY DABBY DOO – it is!

25

The film – *Monster Mash Four* – is totallycompletely-relentlesslydisgustinglyatrociouslymindnumbing-lystunninglypukeinducingly awful.

Thank goodness I never had to sit through the first three.

And the cinema is so decrepit even the fleas have bailed out. No wonder they're planning to knock it down. In fact, if they don't do it soon it'll probably fall down all on its own.

Me and Magnus – who, I have to say, is looking really cool in a midnight-blue shirt and jeans – are sitting as near the back as poss, to avoid the popcorn wars raging in the front.

I'm wearing a neat little skirt I borrowed last week from Cordelia, and at first I think, horrified, five minutes into the film, that Magnus is touching my leg. Then I realize it's not Magnus that's dodgy, thank goodness! It's the seat! There's a spring loose or something and it keeps sticking into me every time I move.

With just the final battle scene to go and only three mutants left alive, Magnus takes my hand and this warm ripply feeling runs right through me and almost makes up for how awful the film is.

When it finishes we stumble, blinking, into the light. A few sad-looking monster-lovers are queuing for the next screening.

Magnus turns to me, his face shining. 'That was brilliant, wasn't it?'

For a moment I think he must be joking, but, no, there's no hint of irony in his voice. He honestly DID enjoy it.

'I'm starving now,' he says, putting his arm round my shoulder. 'I could kill a burger.'

And before I can say anything we're outside the brightly lit glass doors of Meaty MacBurger's.

'Hold on!' I splutter as the glass doors slide automatically open. 'I can't go into Meaty MacBurger's!'

I leap backwards like I've had an electric shock and the glass doors slide shut.

'Why not?' Magnus looks at me, his face crumpled.

'I'm a vegetarian.' I try to say it non-aggressively as I know that some meat-eaters can get a bit upset.

'No problem!' Magnus says. He picks a piece of popcorn from my hair and flicks it into the gutter. And that's when I notice. His eyes are the most extraordinary blue. Bluebell blue. 'You don't have to eat the burger!' he grins. 'It's me that's hungry.'

He steps forward and the glass doors slide open again.

'The problem is,' I begin patiently, reminding myself that this is probably all new to Magnus, 'burgers are made out of cows. And cows eat grass. And grass needs space to grow. And whole acres of Amazonian rainforest are getting burned so they can plant grass so they can feed cows so they can turn them into –'

'Look,' Magnus lets out a huge sigh. 'I just want ONE burger. Not a whole cow. OK? I'm hungry. That's all.'

Minutes later we're inside. I can't bear it. The tinny music. The silly brown and white uniforms with their bullhorn hats. The smiley cow logos.

Magnus places his order. A Super King Size Doubler. He turns to me.

'So what do you want?' He takes a fiver from his pocket. 'I'm paying.'

I stare at the fiver and avoid his eyes. I feel positively squeamious.[24]

'Nothing, thanks. I'll wait outside.'

I am so glad to get out! I take a big deep breath to calm myself. Those boy-hunting hormones

[24] Squeamious = squeamish and nauseous all at once.

must be softening my brain. Pip has had three-day tantrums in the past because I've insisted our family NEVER EVER eats in places like Meaty MacBurger's. Or Florida Fried Chicken.

And Magnus had me in there! Actually IN there.

And that's when I see it. Spray-painted in huge dramatic letters across the town-hall doors.

HANDS OFF BLUEBELL WOOD

In bright green! The same luminous green of the paint can Cordelia found among the ferns. And Twig stuffed in his pocket! Yay! I should have guessed the tree boy would do something like this!

I take out my mobile and switch it to camera mode – just as Magnus emerges from Meaty MacBurger's.

'What are you doing?' Magnus asks, chewing on a mouthful of burger.

'Oh, it's for my art portfolio,' I lie, taking a couple of shots. 'For Miss Cassidy.'

'I can't stand vandalism.' Magnus scowls at the town-hall doors.

'But it's not vandalism!' I protest. 'It's direct action. To save our heritage.'

'Our heritage?' Magnus snorts, as he takes another mouthful of burger.

'Bluebell Wood. Haven't you heard? They're going to chop some of the trees down –'

'Of course they are!' Magnus laughs. 'They're going to chop ALL of the trees down.'

'But they can't!' I gasp. 'Those trees are hundreds of years old. And all sorts of animals live there. Squirrels and foxes and birds and –'

Magnus finishes off his burger, drops the empty wrapper in the gutter and wipes his hands on his jeans. I'm about to protest that he should've found a bin, when he takes both my hands and pulls me towards him.

'Yeah. But guess what we're getting instead,' he says, eyes gleaming like he's got the best ever surprise for me. He hooks his hands round my waist and I look up into his face. Does he really think there's something better than a beautiful old wood, with a stream running through, and trees to climb, and places to have campfires on summer evenings, and squirrels and rabbits and birds and flowers and fresh raspberries?

'Houses or something?' I say, trying not to smell his burger-breath.

Magnus's eyes shine. 'Only a decent cinema, and an ice rink and a shopping mall, and – the best bit of all – an Olympic-size swimming pool! Which means I'll be able to train here without travelling!'

My heart plummets into my shoes. Of course! Why didn't I think of that? They're going to chop down the wood and put a huge concrete mall in its place with a cinema and ice rink and swimming pool all inside it. People have been asking for something like this for years. It all makes a horrible sort of sense.

Crestfallen, I pull away from him. 'How come you know all this?'

'You know how Lovelace is my swim coach?' Magnus grins, really animated now. 'Well, he told me last week. When we were at the time trials in Edinburgh. It's inside info and I'm supposed to keep it quiet. But he won't mind me telling you.' He looks into my eyes and smiles. 'After all, you are my girlfriend.'

26

Magnus walks me home. And all the way he keeps telling me how fab what he calls the new 'mega-mall-multiplex' is going to be.

'When the new pool's open it'll be brilliant! Just think, you'll be able to come along to my time trials and cheer me on,' he says. 'That would be really cool.'

I try to argue about how special the Bluebell Wood is. I even take him into the woods, thinking that way he'll understand.

We walk down the path as dusk is falling. Squirrels go scurrying up the trees. Birds dart through the branches. The place is totally alive. Tiny white flowers glow like fallen stars in the half dark. We stop under an old oak tree that Mum told me when I was little was hundreds of years old.

'Look!' I point out the names cut into the bark, some of them high above us. 'People who'll be dead now once carved their names here. This is part of our history.'

Beneath my feet I can almost feel the heartbeat of the earth. In the distance an owl hoots, ever so softly.

'This place is so special,' I whisper.

Magnus starts laughing, 'Sure, it's great, Sassy. But it's only a wood.'

'Don't laugh! I'm being serious!'

He smiles and puts his arms round my shoulders, his face shadowed in the dying light. 'You're so cute, Sassy. You really are. Especially when you're all het up about something.'

'I am not *cute*,' I say, pulling back slightly.

'You are, Sassy. There's nothing you can do about it. *Cute. Cute. Cute.*' He pulls me closer and my heartbeat starts to race.

'I'm not *cute*, Magnus. Baby seals are *cute*. Little Bambi deer are *cute*. Brown-eyed baby cows are *cute*.'

'Yeah! And Sassy Wilde is cute!'

'No, Magnus, I'm not! *Cute* things are helpless. And they usually end up −'

And I'm about to say 'dead', when suddenly Magnus pulls me forward and kisses me full on the mouth.

And I'm just thinking I wished I'd had some warning so I could've taken a deep breath first and made sure my lips were, well, damp but not slobbery, and I'm also thinking that this is my first real kiss and it's not quite how I'd planned it[25] – when he pulls back and smiles at me again.

'And you're funny,' he says.

'What do you mean, *funny*?'

I'm expecting him to say, you know, that I'm witty and amusing and that's what he finds so attractive, when instead he says, 'You take all this save-the-planet stuff so seriously.'

I stiffen and give him a cold look, but it's like he doesn't register it at all. He just goes burbling on.

'Don't worry, Sass, you'll grow out of it,' he says, stroking my hair and making my spine go all tingly. 'Just like my big sis. One day she was all *Oh, save the dolphins, protect the pandas, honour the ancient oak*, next she was working for the world's biggest oil company! Dad says that's what girls are like. They have all these daft ideas you just have to put up with.'

I pull back and stare at him. What is going on? I mean, this is Magnus. The guy of my dreams, isn't it? Then the awful possibility pokes at the edge of my consciousness. Maybe, just maybe, the Magnus In My Head and the Real Magnus are not the same person?

[25] And I'm thinking it's strange how you can be thinking so many things at once when you don't want to be thinking anything at all!

'Anyway –' he pulls me close again – 'you are cute. There's nothing you can do about it.'

And my brain's shouting, *MAKE IT CLEAR RIGHT NOW, SASS, THAT YOU EXPECT HIM TO RESPECT YOUR VIEWS!* when suddenly he leans forward and kisses me. Again! Even though I really don't want him to! Something Magnus-In-My-Head would never do!

Clumsily I push him back.

'Do you mind!' I gasp. 'First you insult me, then you . . . you . . . you . . .' I'm so furious I can't even find the right word.

'Aw, come on, Sass –' Magnus smiles, catching my arm like he really has not got the message.

I shake my arm free and stare at him, incredulous, and even though it's dark now, it's like I'm seeing him clearly for the first time.

And I don't like what I see.

I give him one last filthy look then turn on my heel and stomp off through the trees towards the main road.

27

I refuse to talk to anyone when I get home.

'How was the film, honey?' Mum asks as she makes hot chocolate for Pip.

'Rubbish,' I mutter. 'I'm going to bed.'

Pip looks up from playing with her Biker Girl Lolitaz. 'So did he kiss you?' she asks, wide-eyed.

'Well, if he did I wouldn't be telling *you*!' I growl. 'You're far too young.'

'Ooooh.' Pip pouts. 'Sorry I asked!' And Mum rolls her eyes. Honestly! I sometimes wonder what Mum is reading in those parental self-help books.

I grab a couple of Mum's freshly made scones piled high with jam, and a glass of milk and the handset from the hall phone, then retreat upstairs to my room. Throwing myself down on my beanbag I phone Taslima. She listens patiently. I can almost hear her eyebrows rising up with professional concern.

'Magnus was UTTERLY out of order,' I

complain. 'I took him into the woods cos I wanted him to see how lovely they are! *And* I thought it would be romantic!'

'Listen, Sass,' Taslima advises, 'you did nothing wrong. Forget Magnus. You need to find a chico who's more like you. You know, someone who's into all the eco stuff.'

Taslima agrees with me that no way should I be made to work with Magnus in biology. So I'm going to ask Mr Hemphead to be paired with someone else. Preferably female. To be honest, I'd even put up with Megan rather than have to partner Magnus.

And by the time I hang up the phone one thing is clear in my head. Next time some chico offers me a bite of his muffin – or anything else – I will most def absolutely completely totally utterly refuse.

I've had enough of boys for a long, long time.

That night I have a weird dream.[26]

It's at some point in the distant future. The Olympics have just finished and Magnus has won seven gold medals. He's Britain's biggest ever swim star. And on account of his male-model good looks he's signed a mega-million-dollar deal

---

[26] Or maybe Cordelia's psychic powers are rubbing off on me, and it's a kind of warning!

with JOCKSTAR, the world's biggest sportswear manufacturer.

And I'm his wife!

It's awful!

I have to go jetting all around the world with him, and my thirty-seven cow-hide suitcases. 'You mustn't worry your pretty little head about the little calves who died to make your luggage,' Magnus says. 'They were killed humanely, and no part of them went to waste. I gobbled it all up in huge mega-big meaty burgers!'

As his cutesy little wife, Magnus insists I have my hair straightened seven times a day by my Filipino maid, Juanita. Juanita is getting paid slave wages, even though we're filthy rich. When I complain Magnus tells me I'm so cute when I get all het up that he loves me all the more.

And we've got a carbon footprint the size of a Third World country! We have all the rooms – in all our mansions – to heat, and our trans-Atlantic flights, and our fully heated Olympic-size swimming pool in our back garden, and our seven cars so Magnus can choose a different one for every day of the week.

'It's the price we have to pay for fame, cutie,' Magnus says as he prepares to leave for another photo shoot. 'Our fans expect it. Now, which car shall I take today, baby?'

I simper, toss my ultra-long, ultra-straight,

ultra-glossy hair, and look all doe-eyed. 'Oh, I don't know, honey . . . maybe the sportster, or the big shiny SUV, or the Humvee . . .'

'You are so cute, princess,' he says, kissing me. Then he's gone. The door slams shut behind him. There's a rattle as a huge key turns in the lock. The grinding of metal on metal as bolts are drawn across. Top and bottom.

I run to the window. I'm ten floors up, in a gilded tower. Far below, Magnus's bright red sportster revs and vrooms off. Our automatic security gates swing open.

The paparazzi waiting outside the gates spot me and the cameras start flashing. Frantically I flap my arms. Help! I can't get out! HELP!

But no one hears me.

They're too far away.

They think I'm waving.

I wake up suddenly and sit bolt upright in bed and switch the lamp on to make my brain stop. I am SO glad I came to my senses about Magnus BEFORE we got married. I can't even imagine now what I first found so attractive about him. Hormones or no hormones, I will NOT be rushing into another relationship.

After a while I tuck down under the duvet again. Exhausted, I drift into dreamless sleep, grateful I have learned my lesson in time.

28

Guess what arrived this morning?

Only a reply – at last! – from the Chief Exec of Paradiso's. You know, about my demand that they stop using plastic bags and plastic packaging on account of the way it's poisoning the oceans?

Mum and Dad, apparently, found the letter funny. But I didn't. I thought it was downright insolent.

> *The Chief Executive's Office*
> *Paradiso's Supermarkets*
> *Milton Keynes*

Miss Sassy Wilde
33 Anton Drive
Strathcarron

Date as postmark

Dear Miss Wilde,

Thank you for your letter regarding the negative impact of plastics on the environment. I have passed your comments to the relevant department.

In the meantime, as you are so obviously fond of fish, can I advise you of our latest special offers? Our dolphin-friendly tuna is currently half price in all our stores, and our fresh farmed salmon is guaranteed at a price lower than any of our competitors.

And, in case of tummy ache, Paradiso's Patented Tummy Soothers should do the trick. I enclose a free trial sample. Satisfaction guaranteed.

Please rest assured you are a valued customer.

Thank you for your concern.

C. J. Sugar
Chief Executive
> *Paradiso's – the supermarket that makes*
> *shopping heavenly!*
> *99.9% of our customers say so!*

Honestly! I'm so furious I could spit! And I'm even more furious that Dad went to Paradiso's last week for his photo shoot. I follow him around the house haranguing him.

'How could you sell out like that?' I demand.

'Sassy, I didn't sell out. It was an excellent opportunity to make some points about environmentally friendly shopping. Read this morning's paper and see for yourself. Paradiso's exists. Some of us have to live in the real world. And,' he adds, flapping the *Strathcarron Herald*, 'there's a lovely photo of you here too.'

He opens the paper at the middle page and hands it to me.

OK, so the headline does say ANGUS WILDE CAMPAIGNS FOR ECO-FRIENDLY SHOPPING. But my eye is caught by the photo of Dad with his arm round me, standing under a big banner: PARADISO'S, WHERE ALL THE BEST PEOPLE SHOP. And I'm about to throw the paper at him and complain that it makes it look like *I* shop at Paradiso's – which I most certainly do not – when the small print underneath catches my eye.

I peer closer.

Parliamentary candidate Angus Wilde with lovely daughter Sasperilla.

'OH NO!' I scream.

Mum looks up from her book. 'What on earth is it now?'

'He's only gone and put my full name in the paper! Now everyone at school will know you called me after a drink and I'll get teased stupid, like forever!'

Dad looks taken aback. 'Oops,' he says. 'That must have been Digby. I wouldn't have done that, Sass.'

I crumple the paper and chuck it at him.

'No! You only gave me the ridiculous name in the first place!'

'Well, actually, it was your mum,' he mutters.

'Yeah! With her mind all unbalanced after childbirth and who knows what drugs! *You* should have been more responsible!'

'Lighten up, Sassy!' Mum says. 'It could have been worse. I might have had a craving for . . . Orangina.'

'Or Fanta,' Dad laughs.

'Or Ribena!' Mum giggles.

'What about Sangria?' Pip shouts through from the kitchen. 'That's a drink, isn't it?'

'Yes, Pip,' I snap angrily. 'An alcoholic drink you're far too young to know about!'

Mum is helpless now, snorting like a demented pig. Her book has fallen to the floor. *The Perfect Mother's Handbook.* I stare coldly at my parents.

'Come on, Sass. Sometimes you have to learn to laugh at things,' Dad says.

But I'm in tears. If Hannah Harrison ever gets a hold of this I will be unable to continue my existence on this planet.

Which is why I am going to my room.

And I may never come out again.

29

Monday morning.

As soon as I walk into the school playground Sindi-Sue comes wiggling over. 'Saw your photo in the paper yesterday,' she says, and my heart sinks. If Sindi-Sue knows my real name now, then everyone – including Hannah Harrison – will know by lunchtime. When it comes to secrets Sindi-Sue's as reliable as a hand-crocheted sieve.

'I never knew your full name was Sasperilla,' she exclaims. 'I don't know why you don't use it. Wish my mum had called me something like that. It's so . . . so . . . exotic.'

'See,' Cordelia laughs as we wait for the first bell to ring. 'Sindi-Sue actually *likes* your name. And I do too. I think it's really cool.'

'And in any case,' Taslima adds, 'if you act like you don't have a problem with it then nobody can tease you, can they? Wind-ups only work if you let them.'

Then the bell rings and we go into registration. Miss Peabody is just taking the register when the door flies open and Mr Smollett strides in, his bald head shining, his black gown flapping, like an extra from a vampire movie.

We all have to stand up and chant, 'GOOD MORNING, MR SMOLLETT.' Apparently he is carrying out a Uniform Spot Check. He passes a beady eye over us. His beady eye stops on me.

'Why are you not wearing a school sweatshirt, girl?' he bellows.

'Mr Smollett, sir, I am,' I correct him.

'You are, are you?' He stares disconcertingly at my chest. 'So where, pray tell me, is the school logo?'

'As a matter of principle,' I explain defiantly, 'I have blacked it out with felt tip.'

'And what principle would that be?' he growls.

'The *No Logo* principle,' I answer. He looks blank. I can see I'm going to have to spell it out for him. 'I refuse to be branded, sir, like a cow in a herd. Or . . . or . . . a pair of Calvin Klein . . . er . . . underwear. I am not a walking advert. For the school or for anything else.'

'What's your name?' he snaps. And I'm about to say Sassy, when I remember what Taslima said earlier. *Act like you don't have a problem with your name, then no one else can tease you with it.*

I take a deep breath and my heart thuds in my

chest. 'MY NAME,' I say, my voice loud and clear, 'IS SASPERILLA WILDE.' The Sasperilla feels kind of odd in my mouth, like it's too big and fizzy, but nothing bad happens. The sky doesn't fall down. No one laughs. There's not even a titter.

'Well, Sasperilla Wilde,' Smollett says, spitting each syllable, 'you can give me a thousand-word essay: "Why Mr Smollett is the Only Principal I Must Obey". I want it on my desk first thing Friday morning.'

'Yes, sir,' I say meekly. But inside I feel anything but meek. This school is nothing better than a malevolent dictatorship! I will do his silly essay. Of course I will. Anything for a quiet life. And, to be honest, I'm relieved he's not going to send a letter home. Cos that would blow the demo disc deal with Dad right out of the paddling pool.

Almost as if he's heard my thoughts Smollett turns at the door. 'Miss Wilde! That essay. I would like it signed by a parent.'

And with that he strides from the room.

Just as well, then, I think as I plop back down on to my seat, that I perfected Dad's signature in Primary Six!

A mad squiggle with a tail. It took me several hours of practice. But hey! I knew it would come in handy sometime!

* * *

I manage to avoid Magnus all morning. Basically, I tell Cordelia and Taslima, I just don't want to see the chico again. Ever. We have nothing in common.

As we eat lunch in the noisy dining hall Taslima suggests I need some time out from the male of the species – including Lovelace in his teensy shorts and Smollett on his boot-camp kick, who is, incidentally giving me the evil eye from the doorway.

'You do know,'[27] says Taslima as she daintily picks the peas from a spicy samosa and pops them into her mouth, 'that in some cultures women have a place of their own . . . like The Ladies' Lodge or The Temple of the Women . . . where men are denied entry. On pain of death. Just so the women can get some peace!'

'Well, actually,' Cordelia says as she finishes off one of her mum's home-made pumpkin pies, 'I didn't know *that*, but my mum's in an all-female coven.'

Just then a banana skin flies across the lunch hall from one of the boys' tables. It splats down just beside Cordelia's lunchbox. Cordelia curls her nose up. 'Personally,' she sighs, 'there are times when I would find a Temple of the Women quite appealing.'

[27] When Taslima says, *You DO know*, it means she's gonna tell you something you most prob DO NOT know.

187

Which is why we head for the girls' loos. The nice quiet ones up at the back of the school. Not exactly a temple, but the best Strathcarron High offers.

Cordelia balances up on the window sill, her little red-shoed feet dangling on the ends of her long white legs and they both listen while I moan again about Magnus.

'Better to find out now he's not the right guy for you,' Cordelia says, in an attempt to soothe my bruised and troubled soul.

'I agree,' says Taslima, who's perched neatly on the pedal bin, making notes in her little pink notebook. 'It would be so much worse if you got married, had kids, then found out, like fifty years later, that he was a dork.'

Just then a toilet flushes – and who do you think emerges from the cubicle, tugging her skirt down? Only Megan!

'Yeah! That's what happened to my mum and dad,' Megan sighs. 'I so wish they'd decided to split up before they met. Mum and me could have been really happy, just the two of us.'

Taslima and me exchange a puzzled look. I mean, if her dad hadn't met her mum she wouldn't exist, right? But Megan doesn't notice.

'If you don't mind me saying so, Sassy, you're well out of it,' Megan continues as she washes her hands.

'You would say that, wouldn't you?' Cordelia blurts. 'Because you fancy the cute little swim pants off Magnus yourself!'

'Past tense,' Megan says flatly, shoving her hands under the drier. 'I learned my lesson at my party. You *do* know what happened, don't you?'

'Not exactly,' Taslima says, her pencil poised to take notes. 'Not from your point of view anyway.'

'Well, we were all playing Spin the Bottle in the lounge. And it was my turn and I spun it and it stopped at Magnus. So we went out to the hall so we could kiss, you know, cos that's what the dare was.' Megan sighs heavily. 'And he kissed me, so I thought, great, cos Cordelia's right, I had fancied him for ages.

'But I was feeling a bit sick – you know – so I went to get a glass of water, and when I came back Magnus had gone! Then I found him in the dining room, and he was chatting to these older guys and I kind of tried to get him to come out to the garden, and, well, in front of everyone he told me to get lost! And I said, well, I thought we were together, what with you kissing me and everything? And he laughed in my face and said it was just a dare. And they were all laughing, so that's why I got so upset and, well –' she takes a deep breath – 'the rest is history.'

'So why did you look so angry every time you saw me and Magnus together?' I ask, confused, recalling all those times I thought I was getting one over on Megan.

'Only because I hate his guts!' Megan exclaims. 'I can't see him without my blood boiling!'

And, of course, that makes total sense to me. Cos I feel exactly the same now.

Taslima looks up from making notes in her book. 'You know,' she says, 'Magnus may be swim champ. He might even be in the top maths and English set. But in the emotional intelligence department he scores a big fat flabby zero.'

'Tell me about it,' Megan sighs. And with that she leaves.

Taslima and Cordelia look at me hard and long.

'What?' I ask.

'Megan must have had a really rough time when her parents split up,' Cordelia says.

'So?'

'So maybe she's over it now. Maybe we should all start being a bit nicer to her.'

'Your parents split up, Cordelia. But you wouldn't steal from your best friend, would you?'

'My parents split up before I was even born, Sassy. I've never known my dad. In fact I don't even know for sure I HAVE a dad![28] So it's no big

---

[28] With a witch for a mother, who knows?

deal. But Megan had to live through her parents' divorce. It must have been really tough.'

'So what are you saying?'

'That what she did to you in primary school was wrong. But maybe it's time to let it go.' Cordelia slips down from the window sill, then drains the last of her cranberry juice and screws the lid back on.

'Is that really bat's blood?' Taslima asks, diplomatically changing the subject. A few red dribbles race down the inside of Cordelia's plastic beaker. She holds it up to the light just as a couple of junior kids wander in.

'Course it is,' she grins, her teeth all stained red. 'Thickened with spider spit.'

The kids look terrified as, cackling wildly, Cordelia, Taslima and I tumble out into the corridor.

All afternoon I keep turning over in my head what Cordelia said. Maybe she's right. Maybe I should be a bit nicer to Megan. Apart from anything else we have a common enemy now. Magnus Menzies.

But it doesn't mean I have to be her friend.

30

I successfully avoid Magnus for most of Tuesday. In biology Mr Hemphead dishes out an assessment test, which means we have to sit, heads down, getting on with it, for the whole period.

Every single time I look up, Magnus is gazing at me like a love-struck pup. I can't believe he didn't get the message on Friday night! It's like he still thinks we're an item.

Last period is PE and Miss Thom, our usual teacher, is off sick today, so our group has to double up with Magnus's. My heart sinks. I can do without him dashing all over the gym, trying to impress the girls with his physical prowess. Like some saddo ape-man.

When Lanky Lovelace breezes into the girls' changing room with his tiny red shorts I try to pull a sicky. But Lovelace isn't having any of it.

'Into your kit, lady! The fresh air will do you good,' he bellows.

'Fresh air?' we all echo, aghast.

'As the delectable Miss Thom is absent today, we're going outside. For one big happy game of football.'

'But it's raining, sir,' Megan says plaintively, as she adjusts her tiny gym skirt.

'Not any more, it's not!' Lovelace grins. 'The rain stopped hours ago. It's a beautiful day!'

'See,' I whisper to Taslima, 'that's what happens when men exercise too much. All the blood diverts to their muscles, and their brain cells, you know, do that atrophy thing.'

'This school's worse than boot camp,' Cordelia mutters. Lovelace turns at the door and frowns at her.

'If you've got something to say, young lady, say it loud, so we can all hear!'

Cordelia smiles sweetly and narrows her green eyes, and for a moment I almost feel sorry for him. He'll probably wake up tomorrow with a giant wart on his nose. Or somewhere worse.

Reluctantly we shuffle out on to the playing fields. It's been chucking it down all morning and the grass is muddy.

'Twice round the track for starters!' Lovelace calls.

We all set off. Suddenly Megan slips and lands heavily on her bottom, her legs in the air. Some of the girls laugh, glad it's her and not them. Some of the boys shout rude comments. And can you believe it? Lovelace just grins. Doesn't even tell them to quit it!

For a moment it looks like Megan might burst into tears and I feel really sorry for her. Me and Taslima rush over and help pull her up. Biting her bottom lip, she mutters a shaky thanks. Her legs are streaked brown with mud. Cordelia magics a paper hanky from nowhere and tries to clean her up. Megan might be my second-worst enemy in the entire universe, but no one deserves to be humiliated. It's just bullying by the back door.

'OK,' Lovelace commands when, panting, we've finished the two laps. 'Line up and we'll get you into teams.'

Ten minutes later a game of football is in full swing. The teams are mixed, boys and girls. The boys are loving it, of course. They're getting to show off. Magnus is in the opposite team from me. Midge Murphy passes him the ball and he dribbles it towards me, skilfully passing one foot over the other, almost dancing.

'Your goal's the other way, Menzies!' Lanky Lovelace shouts. Magnus ignores him. I stand my ground. Suddenly he changes pace and, before I can do anything about it, he NUTMEGS me! Kicks the ball between my legs! Then he picks it up behind me, charges towards the goal and rockets it into the back of the net.

'Nice one!' Lovelace shouts, and his team cheers. Magnus grins at me, like he thinks I'll be impressed. But I'm not. I'm furious.

After what seems like hours, Lovelace blows the whistle for half-time.

A light drizzle is falling and most of the girls are really fed up. Sindi-Sue has broken three of her perfectly manicured nails in an off-the-ball tussle with Beano. There's a big bruise coming up on Megan's leg where Midge kicked her right in front of Mr Lovelace, yet he didn't even award a foul!

And, according to Cordelia, my face is bright purple and my hair's all frizzed up from the sweating and running and rain.

'You look like the wild beast of the jungle!' Cordelia laughs.

'Good,' I say. 'Because I'm going back out there to kick butt.'

Megan looks up from inspecting her bruises. 'I thought you were a pacifist,' she says.

'I am. But that doesn't mean I'm a walkover.'

The whistle blows and we run out on to the field. This half I'm going to mark Magnus. I'll stick to him like superglue. I want revenge for that nutmeg. And Friday night, and all the trees and animals in Bluebell Wood who're going to be killed by people like him who think if they want something they should get it.

Magnus moves forward. I move forward. Magnus moves back. I move back. Out of the blue I manage – in a pure fluke – to intercept a pass from Midge Murphy. Just before Magnus tackles me I slip the ball to Taslima. Taslima passes to Beano. Beano makes a break for it. Magnus gives chase. At the last minute, just as Magnus catches up, Beano flicks the ball to Cordelia, who's standing prettily by the goal mouth.

Cool as you like, Cordelia taps the ball daintily.

Blinded by Cordelia's beauty, the goalie dives the wrong way.

And the ball rolls gracefully into the back of the net.

Magnus is fuming!

'Oh dear,' Cordelia mutters when I run over to hug her. 'Magnus doesn't like losing, does he?'

'I guess not.' I smile.

Then I'm marking him again. The field is really muddy now. Everyone's splattered and slipping about. In front of the goals is a total mud bath. Midge Murphy slips and the ball rolls to Megan's feet.

'Score, Megan! Score!' I scream. She shuts her eyes, kicks wildly – and misses.

The goalie boots the ball up the park and Magnus, jaw set, picks it up just past the halfway line. He starts to drive towards the goal. I hare along behind him. He's about to shoot. I hurl myself forward in a wild sliding tackle. His feet fly from under him, he lifts into the air.

Then SPLAT! He's face down in the mud.

Mr Lovelace gives a huge blast on his whistle, grabs his first-aid kit, rushes past me and falls on his knees beside Magnus. Magnus groans professionally as Lovelace checks him out.

'Don't you realize how valuable this boy is?' Lovelace yells at me. 'He's one of our best athletes. You could have injured him!'

'I didn't see you running over to help Megan Campbell!' I protest, rubbing my shin where a giant bruise is coming up. 'Aren't all pupils in this school equally valuable, sir?'

'Megan Campbell?' Lovelace looks up at me and narrows his eyes like he's working something out. 'Correct me if I'm wrong. But aren't you the girl I stopped outside Mr Hemphill's room? And didn't you tell me that *you* were Megan Campbell?'

Magnus stops groaning long enough to land me in it. 'That's not Megan Campbell.' He fires me a filthy look. 'That's Sasperilla Wilde!'

'It's Sassy,' I spit back. 'Sassy Wilde.'

Lovelace digs into his breast pocket and pulls out a red card. He waves it furiously in my face.

'Go! Wilde! Shower! Now!' he commands. 'Then report to my office!'

I pick myself up. 'Still think I'm cute?' I ask as I brush past Magnus.

Holding my head high, my curly hair bouncing, I limp off towards the school.

And that's when I see Twig. Sitting on the school wall. Grinning.

31

I am absolutely shattered when I get home. Every muscle aches. Lovelace made me do an hour's detention for lying about my name. But at least the parentals don't need to know. Pip's still at her dance class, and Mum and Dad are both out at the Bonny Baby Competition.

I take the radio into the bathroom, run a hot strawberry-scented bath, then lie back in the warm water. I swear I've still got mud in places I didn't even know existed.

I close my eyes and relax. There's a traditional music programme on. Today's Tuesday and the election's on Thursday, so come Friday Dad will have to book my day in a recording studio! I am so happy it's going to happen at last. On my tenth birthday I made this secret five-year plan with a goal for each year.

1. I wanted to get a guitar by the time I was eleven. Which I did.

2. I wanted to learn to play it well enough to sing my own songs when I was twelve. Which I did.

3. And I wanted a demo disc when I was thirteen. Which is on the verge of happening!

I lie soaking in the suds. I wouldn't normally listen to trad music. That's more Mum and Dad's scene, but Miss Cassidy, whose boyfriend's a musician, says I should broaden my knowledge base so I can create my own indie style.

I close my eyes and sink deeper into the hot water. One day I'd like to have my own girl band. I'd still write songs, sing and play lead guitar, but I'd have a drummer, a keyboards player and a bass player. I try to think of a name. Sassy and the Sasperillas. I smile to myself. Maybe I will get used to my name eventually. At least it's not Agnes, or Margaret, or something plain. Then I think up a girl-band name. The Killer Kuties. And guess what we won't sing. Ever. Any stupid love songs.

Just then the music programme ends and the local news comes on.

'*Residents have been celebrating as news of Strathcarron's new mega-mall multiplex has been officially confirmed. Over now to the town hall and the Lady Mayor.*'

'*Of course, we're all sorry to be losing Bluebell Wood, but just look at what we'll be gaining! The new Bluebell*

Centre will house a theatre, swimming pool and all-year-round ice rink. For years residents have wanted better shops, entertainment and sports facilities. We're delighted to be putting this right.'

'So when will work begin, Lady Mayor?'

I sit up straight and water splashes over the edges of the bath.

'Everything's signed and sealed. So why delay? Personally I can't wait to get my skates on.'

'But the community will be losing a green space, won't it?'

'Not at all. The developers have agreed to plant a hundred new trees on the edge of town. So, you see, no one will lose out.'

I grab the radio and turn it off. This is awful. Don't people understand anything about environmental impacts? By cutting down mature trees you lose more than just the trees. You lose beetles and ants and hedgehogs and birds. A whole ecosystem that's taken centuries to build up!

Quickly I shampoo my hair and rinse it. As I rub myself dry with a big fluffy towel I hear everyone coming home.

By the time I get downstairs Pip and Mum are sticking pizzas in the oven and Digby's in the living room on his hands and knees poring over some old maps. Dad's on the phone.

'Yes, I'll hold,' Dad says.

'This new multiplex centre,' I blurt angrily. 'I suppose you've heard where it's going to be?'

Dad sighs and puts his hand over the mouthpiece.

'Yes, Sassy, sweetheart,' he says quietly. 'And I agree it's a problem. The Lady Mayor's obviously pulled it as a pre-election stunt.'

Digby looks up from his map. 'It's proving very popular with the voters. It's going to bring new jobs to the area. Help compensate for the car-factory closure.'

'But what about Bluebell Wood?' I protest. 'Trees are the Earth's lungs. They soak up lots of harmful greenhouse gases. Planting new trees with teensy little leaves doesn't make up for losing big, mature ones.'

Just then Digby's mobile rings. He dives to answer it and disappears into the campaign cupboard.

'Look, Sassy,' Dad says firmly. 'Let us get on with it, will you? The election's two days away. We're doing what we can.'

'So you're just going to give in!' I explode. 'Just because you might lose a few votes!'

'That's enough, Sassy!' Dad orders. 'Getting elected is the priority at the moment. If I win I'll be able to campaign against a whole lot more than just the Bluebell Wood plans.'

Digby reappears. 'Sometimes you have to lose

a battle to win a war,' he says, kneeling down on the floor again.

'Now off you go to your room and play your guitar or whatever it is you do up there!' Dad hisses. 'Just get out of my hair!' He takes his hand from the mouthpiece. 'Hello. Yes, I'm still here.'

'OK, Dad. OK! Keep your wig on,' I mutter and stomp off.

At the top of the stairs I turn and shout, 'By the way, Dad, the guitar's just a cover. I've got boys up here. And drugs. And alcohol. Maybe that's the kind of daughter you'd rather have!'

Mum appears at the foot of the stairs, her reading glasses on top of her head, a bundle of papers in her hand. She looks up at me. 'Sassy, honey,' she says gently. 'Take some time out. Calm down.'

I stomp into my room, slam the door and fling myself down on the bed. I close my eyes and try to find a still, calm place deep inside. Cordelia's been reading this book on Eastern well-being. It explains how if our chakras get out of balance we get ill. Silence and meditation can help balance the chakras, Cordelia says.

So I turn on to my back, flick on my whale songs CD and close my eyes. The sound immediately calms me, the whales singing soulfully, the waves splashing gently. Then I visualize my favourite shade of blue. Cooling, tranquil, peaceful.

I'm just beginning to feel better when this god-awful racket starts up in Pip's room.

Fat chance I have of balancing my chakras with Pip rehearsing her own personal high school musical through the wall. BOOM! BOOM! BOOM!

Moments later I'm hammering on Pip's door. But does she hear? Of course not. And do my crazy parentals who are downstairs planning the take-over of the world – or of Strathcarron, at any rate – do anything to take their wayward child in hand? Of course not! Exasperated, I push the door open.

And stop in my tracks.

The curtains are drawn. Her disco ball spins, casting diamonds of dancing light around the darkened room. Pip's in the centre of the floor, wearing Jamila's tiny glam dress, which I'd got all fixed up to give back to her, and a pair of Mum's stilettos. Pole dancing, like something from late-night MTV – with my old pogo stick!

I switch the light on and she drops the stick. 'What on earth are you doing?' I gasp. Pip stares at me through mascara-laden lashes. 'For God's sake, Pip! You're nine years old. You should be playing houses or climbing trees or . . . something . . . healthy!'

'I'm dancing,' she shouts back. 'Enjoying myself! Something you'd know nothing about!'

I barge over to her music system and unplug it. The music stops abruptly.

'Give me the dress,' I snap. 'It's not even yours.'

She takes it off and throws it at me.

'And the pogo stick,' I demand.

Eyes flashing, she kicks it towards me, then stands, jaw set defiantly, in the middle of the room. In nothing but Mum's high heels, Minnie Mouse knickers and a pink trainer bra.

'You're in MY room,' she screams. 'And I don't want you here. So get out!'

'You know, Pip, you really disgust me,' I say as I pick up the dress and the pogo stick. 'You need to take a long hard look at yourself. And stop watching MTV and reading Lolitaz magazines. They're turning you into a monster!'

With that I storm back to my room and slam the door so hard the basketball ring comes unstuck and falls off. I throw myself on to my bed and bury my face in my pillow.

Maybe, at last, I can get some peace.

32

It's hard when you feel out of step with the whole world. I mean, I know progress has brought lots of wonderful things. We were talking about that in history last week. Without progress we wouldn't have warm houses, we wouldn't have anaesthetics or antibiotics, we wouldn't have clean water. People would die of plagues and famines.

But there's tons of things progress has brought that I can't stand. Like the melting ice caps and climate change and weapons of mass destruction and whole species dying out.

That's what I'm thinking as I sit cross-legged on my rainbow rug, my guitar cradled across my lap.

It's after nine now and starting to get dark, so I've closed the curtains and put my fave blue planet lamp on. It always calms me.

I pick out a few chords. I've been doing a lot of thinking. About me. And the planet. And

Bluebell Wood. Maybe Dad's right. Maybe it's foolish to get into fights you can't win. Maybe sometimes you have to lose a battle so you can win the war.

See, what I'm thinking is this: maybe the only thing I should be aiming for right now is getting my first demo disc out. Then, once I'm famous, I can lead campaigns to save whole rainforests. Like Joan Baez, that folk singer Mum likes. She's really old now but still turns out for demos and gets publicity for all kinds of causes.

Or that ancient French actress who runs an animal sanctuary and campaigns for animal rights and everyone listens to her because she used to be a big star.

Or that supermodel who campaigns against the fur trade.

As these thoughts flit through my brain I gently strum my guitar. And slowly a new song starts to form at the edge of my consciousness.

When the little birds stopped singing
The TV sets were blaring

I reach for my notebook and write those two lines down. There's a melody forming in my head. I sing them softly a couple of times. It sounds good. Gentle and sad. I write down more ideas as they come to me.

Coming up with songs is strange. It's like there's this tap deep inside you that you're trying to turn on. If you can get even a few words, then more start to come. And that's what happens now. Lines start flowing into my head, then down my arm and on to the paper.

Until the night came creeping
And darkness it came seeping
Exhausted people snuggled down to sleep their
  aches away
But the babies started crying
Cos they knew their world was dying
Cos no one stopped the little singing birds
  from going away.

I scribble all the lyrics into my notebook, then try out a simple chord sequence. Playing guitar and making up lyrics always calms me. Like everything outside the song ceases to exist.

Softly I begin to sing. I can see myself in the wardrobe mirror. My hair's dried now, falling about my face in loose tendril curls. And I'm dressed the way I like, in comfy jeans and a little strappy cotton top. For the first time in ages I feel at ease with myself.

As I play I think about all the different kinds of birds who'll lose their homes in Bluebell Wood. Blackbirds and robins. Thrushes and sparrows. Yellowhammers and herons. And as I sing it's almost as if the birds in the tree outside join in.

When I reach the final line, *Cos no one stopped the little singing birds from going away*, I close my eyes and hold the last note, letting it fade. But the birdsong outside continues. A magical sound.

At first I'm amazed. But then it clicks. I cross to the window and swish the curtains open.

And there, among the thick green leaves, is Twig. He grins cheekily and holds up a wooden whistle.

'That was cool,' I say, opening the window wide and leaning out.

'No,' says Twig. 'That song was cool. Really sad. Where did you find it?'

I feel my colour rise. I don't know what to say. I go and get my notebook and show him the page, complete with score-outs.

'Wow! You wrote it?' Twig says, eyes wide.

I nod.

'It's really good.'

And before I can stop myself, I say, 'I know. I'm going to be a star.'

Twig smiles. 'Yeah. That's what Megan said.' He shifts uneasily on the branch. 'It's a bit uncomfortable out here. Can I come in?'

I hesitate. I've never had a boy in my room before. Dad would really freak. And I'm not sure if there's anything embarrassing lying around or not. But right now I'm feeling lonely.

'Why not?' I say, opening the window wide. I hold out my hand to help him in, but he's really agile, and before I know it he's landed on the floor.

I flump on to my bed and settle cross-legged on the rumpled duvet. For some reason I've got this little pleasure feeling, deep in my tummy. Sort of warm and ripply. The crystal mobile tinkles gently in the draught from the open window.

'Cool room,' he says, looking around at the posters of dolphins and polar bears, the butterflies on the ceiling above my bed, the huge illuminated globe lamp on my desk. He runs his eyes over my bookshelves, inspects the titles, pulls out *Silent Spring* and flicks through it.

'I've heard about this. It's one of the first books about pollution and stuff. What's it like?' he asks.

I shrug. 'Heavy going.' I smile. 'But worth it in the end.' Truth is I've never got past the second page.

He slides it back. I hold my breath, hoping he's not going to ask me about *The Revenge of Gaia*. Cos I've not read that either.

Instead he pulls out the first Animals of Farthing Wood book, and I'm thinking, maybe I should say that's Pip's, not mine. I mean, I'm a bit old now for the Animals of Farthing Wood.

'I just love this book,' he says, flicking thoughtfully through it. 'And this is the exact same as mine. Same cover and everything.'

'Yeah,' I say, relaxing. 'I've read it tons of times.'

'And you've got the whole series.' Twig runs his finger along the spines.

'They were my favourites when I was little,' I say.

'Mine too.' He settles cross-legged on the rug and smiles shyly at me.

I've never paid any attention to what Twig looks like before, but now I notice the way his dark wavy hair falls over his soft brown eyes. He's wearing really cool black jeans, a baggy green T-shirt and on one wrist a faded green friendship bracelet. For a moment I wonder if it was a present from someone. A girl maybe.

'You suit your hair curly like that,' he says. 'Straight doesn't look right on you.'

'I know. It was just a phase I was going through.'

'Yeah. I've been through a few of those myself,' he says thoughtfully. 'Like when Mum and Dad were splitting up I went through this heavy grunge phase.'

'You, a grunge?' I gasp. Twig's tanned, a golden

honey brown, like he spends most of his time outdoors. 'You look far too healthy!'

'Yeah, I'm happy just being me now.' He flashes me a white smile. 'It makes life easier.'

As if to signal he doesn't want to talk about himself any more, he gets up and wanders over for a closer look at my Disappearing Rainforests poster. He reads out the quote from the anthropologist Margaret Mead that's printed along the bottom. '*Never doubt that a small group of thoughtful, committed citizens can change the world. Indeed, it is the only thing that ever has.*'

He turns and gazes thoughtfully at me, his head cocked to one side. It's like he's looking right inside my soul.

'You really care about things, don't you?' he asks, his voice soft, gentle.

'It's our world,' I say. 'Grown-ups don't have to care what things are going to be like in fifty years. They just build more factories, churn out more cars, go on more flights. Like that's all that matters. You know, when we're the same age as them, the planet's gonna be a total mess –'

'I know,' Twig says. 'That's why I'm here.'

'I don't follow.'

'If we don't do something they're going to chop down Bluebell Wood –'

'Look, if you want me to ask my dad to help,

forget it. He's already refused. He can't see past the election on Thursday.'

'No, not your dad, Sassy. You.'

'I'm just one person, Twig. I can't do anything on my own.'

'But you won't be on your own,' Twig says, his brown eyes shining. 'There's two of us. You and me. Isn't that what that quote on your poster is all about?'

I laugh. He's so sincere it's kinda funny. 'Look, Twig, we can't save Bluebell Wood. No one can. It's all signed and sealed. It was on the radio. They're starting work right away. It's too late.'

'But don't you see?' Animated, Twig paces the room. 'That's what they want you to think! That you can't do anything. But you can. We can. At the very least we have to try. We can stage a tree-top protest. Tomorrow. Sit up in the trees to stop them chopping them down! Other people have done it. It's worked before!'

I let out a long exasperated sigh. I know all about tree-top protests where eco-warriors sit up in the trees to protect them from developers.

'Look,' says Twig. 'If it's your dad's election chances you're worried about, you needn't. The Lady Mayor's bought everyone off with this new Bluebell Centre. He doesn't stand a chance anyway.'

'Listen, I'm so mad with Dad I couldn't care

less about his election chances. In fact, I kinda hope he doesn't get elected.'

'So what's stopping you?'

'I did a deal with him,' I sigh. 'If I stay out of trouble he'll pay for a demo disc.'

'So?'

'So I don't want to blow my chances, do I? Who knows, I might get a recording contract, and just think: when I'm famous I'll be able to campaign all over the world. Maybe even save whole rainforests!'

Twig looks at me, his eyes suddenly cold. And I know I've let him down. 'That song you sang,' he says. 'It made you sound like someone who cares. But maybe you don't. Not really. Maybe all you care about is you.'

I pick my guitar up and make out like I'm tuning it.

Twig puts one foot up on to the window sill, ready to leave.

'I'm going to be at Bluebell Wood first thing.' Twig steps out on to the branch. 'It'd be good if you were there. But I suppose that's too much to ask.'

I strum my guitar angrily. **STRUM! STRUM! STRUM!**

'Cos you'll be too busy.' He pauses. 'Selling out.'

I stop strumming and look up at him.

'Why don't you just face up to it, Sassy,' he says. 'Fame's what you really want. You'll pay whatever price you have to, just so you can be a star.'

And then he's gone.

33

I am so rattled! I feel as irritable as a snake who needs to shed a skin.

I bang my window closed and tug my curtains tight shut, then go downstairs to get a drink.

How dare Twig accuse me of selling out! Who's he to come over all holier-than-thou?

Boys really are more trouble than they're worth! Mr Hemphead says some creatures, like slugs and starfish, don't need mates to reproduce. They just do it all on their own. Mr Hemphead says they're called hermaphrodites. Maybe that's what Cordelia's mum is. And, right now, that's what I'd like to be. A hermaphrodite. I mean, who needs chicos?

'Everything OK, honey?' Mum asks when I bang the fridge door shut. She's just made a tray of flapjacks, all sweet and sticky. 'You can have one if you want,' she says, smiling. 'Go on. You know you love them.'

I turn my head away. 'No thanks. I'm not hungry,' I mutter.

Mum pulls up a chair. 'Come on, sweetie. Give.'

I breathe in deeply but keep my lips tight shut.

'You'll feel better if you talk about it,' she persists.

'I won't,' I say as I leave the room. 'Nothing will make me feel better. Ever.'

The big grandfather clock in the hall booms as I pass. And gives me a brilliant idea! I shall rewind my memory clock to an hour ago. To before Twig turned up. You can do that with computers if they hit a problem. You choose an earlier time and date to restore them to. I will restore my life to the pre-Twig point when I'd just worked out my perfect plan.

In my room I pick up my guitar again. Softly I play the opening chords for 'When the Birds Stopped Singing'.

I open my notebook at the page and start to sing.

> When the little birds stopped singing
> The TV sets were blaring
> The cars were roaring up and down the busy
> motorways

It doesn't feel right. The words stick like sawdust in my mouth.

There's no birdsong. No Twig. The song sounds totally rubbish. I hurl my notebook across the room. It thuds off the rainforest poster and, like a wounded bird, falls, white pages fluttering, to the floor.

I'm exhausted. I can't get to sleep. My chakras are all in a knot, like a big ball of tangled wool, and it's too late to phone Taslima for advice. I lie in the dark, staring at my luminous butterflies, for what feels like several years, but when I check the time it's only ten o'clock.

It's one more day till the election. Two days till I can book a recording studio. *Two days*, I tell myself, *is not that long*. Then again it's forty-eight hours. Which is 2,880 minutes. Or 172,800 seconds.

172,799 seconds.

172,798 seconds.

172,797 seconds.

I pull my duvet tight up round my ears. My pillow feels like a brick. I sit up and pummel it with my fists, unable to decide whether it's Twig or Magnus.

I lie down again. Spit! Spit! Spit! Why did I have to think of Magnus and Twig again? Why don't they just get out of my brain? There's not enough room in there for them. Honestly, it's like they're haunting me.

Brainwave! I'll do that thing Taslima suggested to get rid of unwanted memories. I visualize a beautiful island. There's a rowing boat tied up by the edge of a huge blue ocean. I put Magnus and Twig in the boat, untie it from the shore and push it off firmly. It floats out gently. 'Bye, Magnus! Bye, Twig!' I call happily as they drift further and further off into the distance. And I'm just thinking, *That's fine. I have dealt with them*, when suddenly this wind gets up and the tide turns and the boat starts coming back. Then Twig sits up, grabs a big pair of oars and starts rowing like crazy back towards the shore. I watch in horror as the boat draws closer, then Magnus dives into the water and starts swimming towards me!

I sit up suddenly. My tummy rumbles really loudly. Of course! No wonder I can't get to sleep! I've hardly eaten today. I remember Mum's flapjacks. Why did I refuse to take one? They'll be in the fridge. A couple of them and a glass of milk should send me off to the Land of Nod no problem.

Yawning, I slip out on to the landing. And trip over a fat big box dumped outside Pip's door. What on earth has she been up to now?

Curious, I open it and rummage inside. First

I pull out several Lolita Dollz. Then Pip's Ballroom Barbie with her big purple sticky-out dress. Pip wept for three solid weeks to get that! I delve deeper and tug out more Lolitaz, her sequinned disco-dancing leotards, the little diamante dance shoes she got from Santa. At the bottom I find her make-up bag and her hair straighteners. Then I notice 'CHARITY SHOP' scribbled on the side of the box in Pip's big wobbly letters.

I shove everything back in, fold the lid shut and tap gently on Pip's door. She doesn't answer, so I push it open enough to stick my head round.

Pip's all tucked up in bed, lying on her side, eyes wide open, sucking her thumb the way she used to when she was tiny.

'Why have you put all your things out?' I ask softly.

'I don't want them any more,' she mumbles into her pillow. Then she sniffs. And I realize she's crying.

I pull the box inside and sit on the edge of her bed. 'But those are all the things you love best, Pip. You can't throw out your leotard and shoes! What will you wear when you go to dance class?'

'I'm not going back to dance class,' she sobs. 'And I'm not going to ask for new things any more. Ever. I'm going to be all eco-friendly. Like you, Sassy.'

'Oh, Pip,' I whisper, stroking her hair. 'Is this because I was angry earlier?'

Her thumb still in her mouth, she nods. A big tear rolls down her cheek. Oh no! I feel dreadful. What have I done?

'I don't want you to be like me, Pip,' I say gently. 'It'd be a really boring world if everyone was the same. I just want you to be yourself. And your self likes being pretty and wearing pink and disco dancing.'

Pip looks up at me, her eyes huge and shiny with tears. 'But you don't like me,' she sobs.

'I do, Pip. I love you. Exactly the way you are. It's me I don't like. You're fun and sweet, and I know you didn't mean any harm. I just didn't like seeing you dancing like that. It made me angry. But it wasn't just you I was angry with. I was angry with me as well.'

'You still like me?'

'Course I do,' I say, giving her a big hug. Then I dab her cheeks dry and tuck her duvet tight around her. 'You're my little sis, Pip,' I whisper into her hair. 'Just don't try to grow up so fast.'

I sit with her for a while till her eyes close and her breathing steadies. And I'm about to stand up slowly and tiptoe to the door when she sits up suddenly and grabs my arm.

'Sassy, you won't let the bad men chop down Bluebell Wood, will you?' her voice quivers.

'I can't stop worrying about all the little animals. All the birds and squirrels. And the fox that comes and steals Brewster's bones. They'll all be homeless if the trees go.'

I gaze into her eyes. A little innocent girl who trusts her big sis to do the right thing.

'Of course I won't let the bad men chop down Bluebell Wood,' I say quietly.

'Thanks, Sassy,' she sniffs, snuggling back down under the duvet. 'You're the best big sis ever. I think I can sleep now.'

34

What have I done?

Why make a promise I can't keep?

I drop, exhausted, on to my bed and lie listening to the mystical tinkling of my crystal mobile moving gently in the night breeze.

Maybe because I know I can't sit back and do nothing? Because I know that what makes my songs good, what makes me good at singing them, is that they come from the heart. If I betray my heart I can have the best singing voice in the world but it'll count for nothing.

I sit up and switch on my illuminated globe. It looks especially beautiful at night. Almost like it's the real Earth floating out in the vast darkness of the universe. The blue planet. The most beautiful planet. I spin it a few times. And think.

Twig, dammit, is right. Even if you're the only one, you've got to at least try.

But he's wrong too. One boy in one tree is not

going to stop developers with pound signs spinning in their eyes.

I'm still awake when I hear Digby leaving, then Mum and Dad locking the doors, switching the lights out, coming up to bed, laughing and chatting quietly.

I slip out of bed and pick my notebook up from where it fell. Some of the pages are badly crushed. I smooth them out and make a few quick notes.

When I'm sure Mum and Dad are asleep, I creep downstairs and into Dad's campaign cupboard. At the press of a button his computer whirrs into life. I open a new document and start typing. Thank goodness the parentals are sound sleepers.

An hour later I'm finished. I switch the computer and printer off, gather up the huge pile of paper and, yawning, my eyes heavy, pad back upstairs to bed.

Almost immediately I fall asleep.

I'm sure I've only been in bed five minutes when my alarm goes off. Next thing Mum's shouting, 'Are you awake, Sassy?'

I rub my eyes and blink at the light. Whoever said being an eco-warrior would be easy?

Just then Pip sticks her head round my door, skips across and leaps on to my bed. She gives me a great big hug, then boogies downstairs for breakfast.

I shower quickly. Back in my room I take the bundle of flyers I printed off last night and have one last read through.

HANDS OFF BLUEBELL WOOD
SAVE our ancient woodland!

JOIN

SCHOOL WALK-OUT

AND MASS SIT-IN
AT BLUEBELL WOOD

STOP THE DEVELOPERS
stealing our trees

Meet at MAIN GATE TODAY
when second bell rings.

I close my eyes for a moment. My tummy feels full of butterflies – all of them in a panic. I am taking such a risk here. Dad is going to be furious. And I'm really, really sorry that if this comes off he'll probably lose the election for having such an out-of-control kid. But I'm sacrificing something too. I'll NEVER get my demo disk now. In fact I'll be lucky if Mum and Dad don't put me up for adoption. But at least I won't have sold out.

I tip all my schoolbooks on to the floor, stuff the flyers inside my backpack and fasten the clips.

'Sassy! There's a Sassy Special Smoothie here for you!' Mum shouts up the stairs.

A few minutes later I stroll into the kitchen, trying to act like this is a day like any other. Mum passes me the smoothie and, even though my insides feel like a mad scientist took them all out last night and put them back in the wrong places, I attempt a few sips.

'I do NOT believe it!' Dad exclaims from the campaign cupboard. 'We're clean out of printer paper. How did that happen?'

Mum puts down her book, *The Frazzled Mother's Survival Guide*, and rolls her eyes. 'Keep out of your dad's way, girls. It's the last day of the campaign. Tense stuff. Nerves are getting the better of him.'

'No worries.' I smile weakly, leaving the unfinished smoothie on the draining board. 'I'll keep well clear.'

'And the printer ink's out too!' Dad yells.

'I'm off,' I say to Mum, grabbing my backpack.

'I don't blame you,' Mum sighs. 'Wish I could come with you!'

35

I jog all the way to school, adrenalin pumping through my veins.

A few early kids are milling about in the playground. The doors are kept locked until the first bell as a security measure. Apparently to stop Mad Rambo Psychos roaming the corridors. Uh? Like Mad Rambo Psychos couldn't just as easily roam the playground – where we all have to stand about and wait!

Just then Miss Cassidy's little pink Ka rolls into the car park and she gets out, smoothing down her flowery purple skirt. Of course! I dash across to meet her.

'Miss, miss, I'm really desperate for the loo,' I say, hopping frantically from foot to foot, my face contorted. 'Could I just slip in with you? Please?'

'Oh, you poor thing,' she says, rummaging in her big velvet bag for her electronic pass. 'Of course I'll sneak you in. Just don't tell anyone it was me. OK?'

Seconds later I'm inside!

'Thanks, miss!' I grin, then scoot along the corridor towards the loos.

But I don't go anywhere near the toilets. Instead I tug the stack of flyers from my backpack, then dash in and out of the registration rooms, scattering them on the desks.

I have to be quick. I've got about ten minutes till the first bell goes. Most of the teachers usually wait in the staffroom till the crush of kids is over. I'm counting on the kids getting into the rooms first and having time to read the flyers. The minute the teachers get their hands on them they'll most likely bin them.

I've got the first two floors done and hardly any flyers left. Taking the stairs two at a time I zip up to the third floor. The senior common room is at the far end. I leg it along the deserted corridor. Suddenly there's a shout behind me.

'You! Girl! What are you doing?'

I freeze. Lovelace! Just my luck. I'm about to turn to face him when this little voice says, 'Why? Why not make a run for it? You can't be in any more trouble than you are already!' So I take off like a greyhound from a trap, burst through the swing doors and batter down to the next floor.

Lovelace's footsteps come thundering behind me. I dash into the bottom corridor. I don't really know where I'm going. Like a fox being chased by a hound I'm running blind, fear powering my legs.

Just then the bell rings. Pupils flood in through the doors, jostling, laughing, joking. I get caught up in the flow, just one more kid in uniform among hundreds. Behind me Lovelace is screaming, 'STOP THAT GIRL! NOW!'

And kids are turning, wondering what all the fuss is. My lungs feel like they're going to burst, so when this huge Sixth Year guy with bleached blond hair grabs me I don't even try to resist. He's miles bigger than me anyway. And stronger.

So that's it, I think, *the game's up.* When suddenly, with an almighty shove, he bundles me through a door and slams it shut behind me.

I look around. It takes me a few seconds to realize where I am. The boys' toilets! Aaarghhh! Thankfully there's no one using the urinals. And I'm thinking it's as well the place is empty when there's the sound of flushing from a cubicle! My heart sinks. I am SO embarrassed. Then the door opens, and out wanders . . . Magnus?!

He stares at me, astonished. Outside in the corridor Lovelace is still pacing up and down bellowing, 'Who saw her? Sassy Wilde! Which way did she go?'

A babble of voices is shouting different things

at him. '*She went down the stairs, sir.*' '*She went up the stairs, sir.*' It's obvious everyone's doing their best to confuse him.

Magnus starts washing his hands. 'You know, Sassy,' he says quietly, 'you're right. You're not cute at all. Hanging about in the boys' toilets now? You're barking mad!'

'You're not going to tell Lovelace, are you? Where I am, I mean,' I whisper.

Magnus shakes his head. 'I'm not a snitch,' he says, then he goes back out into the corridor, shutting the door firmly behind him.

I slide to my hunkers and look at my watch. People will be picking up the flyers now. Reading them. Talking about them. I suppose some kids will get angry and argue that, if it's a choice between a new centre and some old trees, they'd rather have the centre. Some might remember the good times they had playing in the woods when they were little, building dams across the stream, feasting on wild brambles and raspberries, catching tiddlers in the burn.

Waiting in the chilly, eerie silence, my OI[29] starts to whirr into action. To control it I set my brain a sum.

In Sassy's school there are 523 pupils. If one pupil in

[29] Overactive imagination. Remember?

every ten decides to walk out, how many will be at the
school gate at ten past nine?

Answer: 52.3

Time passes slowly. I prepare myself for the
worst possible scenario.

*In Sassy's school there are 523 pupils. Nine are off
sick. Three are dogging it. One is on permanent exclusion.
If all the pupils in school, except Sassy, decide to stay in
class how many pupils will be at the school gate at ten
past nine?*

My tummy feels all knotted up. I feel sick. I
wonder if this is what the Greenpeace activists
felt like just before they broke through the perim-
eter fence to try to stop them building that huge
new airport terminal in London?

At nine minutes past I slowly open the door to
the corridor and stick my head out. Good! There's
no one about. I dash for the fire exit where
Cordelia, Taslima and me like to sit. Moments
later I'm out in the fresh air. I take a deep breath.
There's no going back, Sassy! You are an
eco-warrior! You are brave and fearless and will
die for what's right!

It feels very lonely as I jog across the playground. I imagine Smelly Smollett at his office
window, glaring through binoculars, waiting to
spot and identify latecomers, and seeing me
instead, heading the wrong way.

Seconds later I'm at the gate, my heart

hammering as hard as a hyperactive metronome. I close my eyes and take a few deep calming breaths, then force myself to look back at the school buildings.

The bell rings.

Cordelia's first to appear, her red ribbons bobbing as she strides towards me, grim-faced. Megan's just behind, dragging a confused-looking Sindi-Sue. They form a circle around me.

'Thanks, guys,' I say. 'I really appreciate this.'

'We can't let them chop down Bluebell Wood,' Megan says. 'It's a sacred burial site. Remember? Our My Little Ponies are buried there.'

Cordelia hugs me tight. 'It's weird, Sassy,' she says. 'I must be losing my powers. I didn't see this coming.'

A couple of Sixth Years – the big guy with the bleached hair and a girl with braids – come out next. Then Taslima and Beano and Midge Murphy! My heart lifts. I'm not going to be on my own!

A straggle of seniors streams noisily out of the science block and heads towards us. Mr Hemphead trots behind them, and can you believe it? He's wearing an orange jumper! Suspiciously like the one Miss Peabody's been knitting forever.

'Are you sure you want to do this, sir?' I ask,

taken aback. 'Won't Mr Smollett expel you or something?'

'New jumper, new start,' Mr Hemphead shrugs. 'To be honest, I've had enough of being a teacher. There must be better things to do.'

There's a whole group of kids around me now.

'We should get going,' Cordelia says, nodding back towards the school. She's right. Mr Smollett, purple as an aubergine, is tanking towards our raggle-taggle band of renegades, his black gown flapping like the Angel of Death.

'Let's get outside the school walls!' the girl with hair braids urges.

Quickly we crowd through the gate. At least twenty, maybe even thirty of us. Smollett stops in his tracks.

'OK, everyone,' I call, my voice quivering with adrenalin and excitement, 'this is the plan. When we get to the woods, we climb into the trees nearest the road. That's where they'll try to get any machinery in. Let's go!'

'SASPERILLA WILDE!' Mr Smollett roars from the other side of the school wall. 'GET BACK IN HERE THIS MINUTE!'

As we turn and stride away Cordelia takes my hand and squeezes it tight. 'Don't worry,' she says. 'It'll work out fine. I've got this hunch.'

Smelly Smollett shouts again, but I don't care.

And I don't care what he threatens me with. As I walk away I work out the latest worst-case scenario:

1. I get excluded from every school forever.
2. My parents divorce me.
3. I am locked up in a secure unit for out-of-control eco-warriors and I never see daylight again.

But, whatever happens, I'll just have to deal with it. There's no going back now.

Minutes later we arrive at the woods. Twig's already there, just like he said he'd be! He's perched high in the branches of the big old beech tree and he grins and waves when he sees us coming. My heart flips over happily. I know now I'm doing the right thing.

Twig looks down from the branches, his face shining, as more and more of us arrive. Quickly I organize people into different trees.

Some of the girls are really struggling to climb up, even on to the lowest branches, but the older boys hoist them up manfully. Sindi-Sue breaks a nail. And – can you believe it – she laughs! The Sixth Year guy with the bleached blond hair – the one who shoved me into the boys' loos – comes to her rescue and helps her into the branches of an oak tree. Sindi-Sue smiles down at him and pats the branch beside her. 'There's plenty of room for two,' she simpers. Trust Sindi-Sue! She's turned an environmental protest into an opportunity to land a fella!

Almost everyone's settled in a tree now. It looks strange. And lovely. Like the trees have blossomed with people. Mr Hemphead looks like a big orange fruit. I'm the last person on the ground. I look up at Twig.

'There's space up here,' he grins.

Minutes later I'm perched beside him.

'I brought this for you,' he says shyly, thrusting what looks like a neatly folded tablecloth into my hands.

'How did you know I'd come?'

'I'm psychic,' he smiles.

'What is it?' I ask, puzzled, turning the cloth over.

'Open it out and see,' he says. 'Give me one end. You take the other.'

We spread ourselves out along the branch.

'OK!' Twig says. The cloth drops open. There's a moment's silence. Then everyone cheers and whoops and claps. I have to half hang off the branch to see why. It's amazing! It's a protest banner. At the top, in big black letters, it says:

SAVE BLUEBELL WOOD

In the centre there's a black-rimmed coffin – full of beautiful bluebells, their little heads hanging sadly. He's even done a border of flowers and butterflies and birds in all the colours of the rainbow.

'It's great, Twig,' I say, straightening up again. 'It's art.'

Just then everyone falls silent as a workers' lorry, loaded with chainsaws and ropes, pulls up.

'Looks like you got here just in time,' Twig says quietly.

The workmen jump down from the cab and look up, confused, at the faces staring down from the trees.

'You may as well go away,' I shout. 'We won't let you cut any trees down!'

The men shrug at each other and the older one takes out a mobile phone and makes a call. For what seems like ages he argues with someone on the other end of the phone. His mate leans on the lorry and lights a fag. Then Mr Hemphead, who's usually so quiet, starts up a chant.

'HANDS OFF BLUEBELL WOOD! HANDS OFF BLUEBELL WOOD!'

The chant grows louder and louder as more people join in. Motorists passing on the road hoot their horns. The man on the mobile cups a hand over one ear, like he's having difficulty hearing. He looks exasperated. Then he holds the phone up towards the trees. 'HANDS OFF BLUEBELL WOOD!' we all chant even louder than before.

Twig turns to me and smiles nervously. 'Here goes, Sassy. The battle has begun!'

36

After the men get back into their truck and drive off there's a party atmosphere. People produce packets of crisps and chocolate bars and apples and bananas from their backpacks. Cans of juice are passed around too. And Mad Midge, who's usually a brain-free zone, surprises us all by offering to go to the nearest shop with Beano to make sure we have tons of supplies for the rest of the day.

After a while everyone starts to go quiet. The girl with braids climbs down from her tree and clambers up beside me and Twig.

'What do we do now?' she asks.

My heart sinks. I'd only thought of getting people here. What are we going to do now? Stay up in the trees forever? For a split second I have this horrible image of Twig and me sitting on this branch, our hair all long and straggly and grey, our faces wizened, our clothes in tatters.

Then Mr Hemphead shouts, 'Why don't we sing a protest song?'

'Yeah!' the Sixth Year guy with bleached blond hair calls. 'I know one!' and he starts up, '*We shall not, we shall not be moved, we shall not, we shall not be moved . . .*' and everyone joins in.

In the middle of the song I notice Megan climbing quietly down from her tree and disappearing into the woods. It doesn't surprise me really. I was amazed she'd come along in the first place.

The singing tails off suddenly when a huge black shiny limousine with tinted windows pulls up at the edge of the road.

'It looks like a hearse,' Cordelia laughs. Sindi-Sue looks confused. 'You know,' Cordelia explains. 'The special car thing they take the coffin to the graveyard in. I'm going to have a horse-drawn one, black and gold, pulled by two black stallions with huge feathered plumes.'

'At least that'll be eco-friendly,' Twig comments, 'which is more than can be said for that huge petrol-guzzler.'

We're all trying to be light-hearted, pretending we're not bothered, but the air feels tight with tension. Even the birds have fallen silent.

A uniformed chauffeur jumps out. He walks round and pulls the rear door open. A tall, thin woman in a suit slides out and straightens her skirt. She stares at our banner, then raises her gaze higher and looks, with a piercing blue gaze, straight at me. It's the Lady Mayor.

'Don't I know you?' she asks, smiling coldly. 'Don't tell me! Yes, you're Angus Wilde's girl. I never forget a face. It's Sassy, isn't it? Sassy Wilde.'

She's trying to make out we're old mates, that we can sort this out. I do my best to avoid her gaze. There's something about her. Like that scary Medusa woman with the snakes for hair. If you look into her eyes you'll be turned to stone.

'Now, Sassy, perhaps you and your friends would like to come down?' she says pleasantly, as if all she's got to do is ask, and like good girls and boys we'll bow to her authority, do her bidding.

'I don't think so,' I call out bravely, 'because if we do you'll just move in and chop all the trees down.'

'Not at all, Sassy. If you come down, then we'll all go back to the town hall, have some juice and sandwiches and talk things over –'

'You can't bribe us like that!' I protest. 'We've got our own juice and sandwiches!' And Midge Murphy waves the big bag of stuff he brought back from the shop. The Lady Mayor shoots him a withering look. It doesn't work. Midge Murphy's immune to withering looks. He's spent his life deflecting them.

The Lady Mayor returns her cool gaze to me and smiles, but there's something missing from the smile now, some assurance.

'We don't need to talk,' I say, as loud as I can, so everyone can hear. 'If you sign a properly witnessed, legally binding statement promising that Bluebell Wood will be protected from development – forever – then we'll come down.'

'Quite the little politician's daughter, aren't we?' she says, an edge of ice in her voice. She turns as if to go, then stops and looks back.

'You do realize this will ruin your father's election chances, don't you? I had expected better of you,' she pauses. 'And I'm sure he did too.'

Tears sting the backs of my eyes. I don't mind getting into trouble with the school. I don't even mind getting into trouble with the police. They can lock me up forever, they can even burn me at the stake, like Joan of Arc.[30] I'm prepared to die for what I believe in. But the thought of ruining things for Dad makes me feel absolutely wretched.

[30] I have concerns, however, about the carbon emissions from burning people at the stake. Might have been OK in the Middle Ages. But hardly environmentally acceptable in this day and age.

'Sassy's doing what she knows is right,' Twig shouts angrily. 'Not like some people.'

I fight back my tears and find my voice again.

'This isn't about my dad, Lady Mayor. It's not even about me. Or you. It's about the animals who live here – the birds and the squirrels and the beetles and the butterflies. It's about children who aren't even born yet having green spaces –'

'Yeah!' Cordelia butts in. 'To bury their My Little Ponies in!' And everyone laughs.

'So maybe you don't care what we think because we're not old enough to vote. Well, maybe we don't have votes, but we do have consciences. And our consciences tell us to do what's right!'

'Go, Sassy, go!' Beano shouts, punching the air.

'You tell her, kid,' the girl with braids shouts.

Then Cordelia starts up the chant. 'HANDS OFF BLUEBELL WOOD! HANDS OFF BLUEBELL WOOD! HANDS OFF BLUE-BELL WOOD!' and the Lady Mayor, her face stony with anger, strides back to her limousine and climbs in.

Just then, to our astonishment, Miss Cassidy and Miss Peabody and more kids from the school arrive!

'We've decided to join you,' Miss Peabody shouts up to us. She looks around at the protestors perched in the trees and smiles happily. 'Reminds me of my student days! I was at Greenham Common, you know. Knitted seven jumpers in my time there. Oh, and three scarves. And a tea cosy.'

Mr Hemphead, who's grinning like a lovesick thirteen-year-old, leans down and hauls her up beside him. Beano and Midge and the crew start whistling and cheering and Mr Hemphead blushes as orange as his jumper.

Miss Cassidy stands below our tree and casts a critical eye over Twig's banner.

'Miss Cassidy's our art teacher,' I whisper to Twig.

At last she steps back and beams up at him. 'You're really talented.'

'I know,' he says, and we both laugh.

Then Miss Cassidy takes a mobile out of her big velvet bag and takes photos of the banner and us. We shout, 'HANDS OFF BLUEBELL WOOD!' a few times especially for her.

'Miss,' I say, when things go quiet again. 'About telling you a lie this morning. You know, to get into the school. I'm sorry.'

'No sweat, Sassy,' Miss Cassidy says. 'It was all for a good cause.'

And that's when Megan reappears and, to my

amazement, she's carrying my guitar! She stops under my tree and looks up.

'I hope you don't mind. I climbed in your window, you know, the way we used to. I've been wanting to say sorry about using your poem.' She passes the guitar up to me. 'I wanted to do something to make up for it. I think you should sing one of your songs.'

'So do I!' Twig says, grinning. 'Nice one, Megan.'

Megan fires him a look. 'Did you just pay me a compliment?'

Twig laughs. 'Yeah, stepsis. I do believe I did.'

'Thanks, Megan,' I say quietly. 'Let's forget about the poem now. We were both kids then.'

'You sure?' she asks.

'I'm sure.'

'Sing us a song, Sass!' Midge Murphy shouts.

'Go on, Sassy,' Miss Peabody calls. Then she turns to Mr Hemphead. 'She's really good, you know.'

I tuck my end of the banner under my bottom so I can have my hands free to play. Then, quickly, I start tuning my guitar. And almost fall out of the tree!

'Steady, Sassy!' Megan shouts from a branch opposite. 'You're supposed to wait till AFTER your first hit before you kill yourself!'

I strum a few chords then take a deep breath. My third public performance. I begin to sing, softly at first, and everyone falls silent.

When the little birds stopped singing
The TV sets were blaring
The cars were roaring up and down the busy
    motorways
The telephones were ringing
The checkout tills were pinging
And no one noticed that the little birds had
    gone away.

Until the night came creeping
And darkness it came seeping
Exhausted people snuggled down to sleep their
    aches away
But the babies started crying
Cos they knew their world was dying
Cos no one stopped the little singing birds
    from going away.

When I finish everyone whoops and claps, and someone shouts, 'Give us another song, Sassy!'

I look at Twig and he nods. I know exactly the one to do next. It's loud and it's angry.

'This one's for the trees,' I say. Then I strum a few loud chords and go for it.

Don't put your axe to my throat
Don't spray toxic fumes in my face
The world is a beautiful place
And in it there's plenty of space
For the fishes that swim in the ocean
And the birds that nest high in the trees
There's room for the whales and the dolphins
For the spiders and beetles and bees.

Don't spoil it, don't kill it, don't waste it
Don't use it, abuse it, pollute it
Don't chop it, don't harm it, don't shoot it
Don't spoil it for you and for me . . .

Suddenly a police car comes roaring towards the wood, sirens blaring, lights flashing, and screeches to a halt. To our amazement Mr Lovelace steps out, complete with the megaphone he usually uses for school sports.

He walks over and plants his legs, arms akimbo.

'This is a message from Mr Smollett,' his voice booms. 'Come back to school NOW and you will be treated leniently!'

'Treated *what*, sir?' Sindi-Sue shouts, like she doesn't know what 'leniently' means. Everyone laughs. Lovelace looks furious.

'As I said,' he repeats, 'if you come back to school NOW and report to the assembly hall, there

will be NO SERIOUS REPERCUSSIONS.'
Then he drops the megaphone from his mouth
and says, so only those nearest will hear, 'Except,
of course, for the ringleaders.'

'RINGLEADERS?' Twig yells. 'WHO ARE
THEY?'

Lovelace throws him a look as hard as a fist,
then shifts his gaze along the branch to me. 'They
know who they are,' he says, eyes narrowed.

'What if we're all ringleaders, Arthur?' Miss
Peabody shouts, and everyone laughs and cheers.

'Yeah! I'm a ringleader!' Sindi-Sue's new boyfriend shouts from the branches of the oak tree.

'Me too!' A girl's voice this time.

'And me!' another voice rings out. Then another
and another, until everyone's shouting at once.
'I'M A RINGLEADER! I'M A RINGLEADER!
I'M A RINGLEADER!'

'Have it your own way!' Lovelace bellows
through his megaphone.

As he turns on his heel Cordelia starts up the
chant again: 'HANDS OFF BLUEBELL WOOD!
HANDS OFF BLUEBELL WOOD!'

I eye the police officers and hug my guitar tight.
If I'm going to be pulled down from the tree I
don't want it damaged in any way.

'Calm down,' Twig says, seeing the panic in
my eyes. 'They're not going to storm us. They
wouldn't dare. Look!'

A white van with blacked-out windows and a satellite dish on top is pulling up behind the Lady Mayor's limo. A couple of men and a woman climb out. Then I see the logo on the side of the van. It's the TV news team!

'It looks like we really are going to be famous,' Twig chuckles.

37

Half an hour later there are cars parked all along the road. Some parents have heard what's going on and have turned up to shout encouragement to their kids and bring them more supplies. The Lady Mayor has done a brief interview with the TV crew and has retreated again into her car. The police are standing around, enjoying the sunshine. A couple of journalists are leaning against their cars, smoking, and photographers have turned up from the newspapers and photographed Twig's banner.

'So what are your demands?' one of the journalists shouts up to Twig and me.

'We want them to leave Bluebell Wood alone,' I call down.

'You're saying you don't want a new mall? A new cinema, swimming pool, ice rink?'

Just then another car drives up. I recognize it right away. It's Digby's little Metro. He unfolds himself from the driver's seat. The blood freezes in my veins as Dad climbs out too.

The Lady Mayor homes in on him. 'Not before time, Mr Wilde,' she says loudly. 'Perhaps you can talk some sense into that girl of yours and get her to call off this silly protest.'

My stomach clenches. Dad looks grim-faced. Digby's eyes shine manically. I want to tell Dad how sorry I am. I know I've lost him the election. And he's put so much work into it. I feel sick that I've let him down.

Dad turns and looks at the banner. Then he raises his gaze and looks directly at me. The colour drains from my face.

'No, Lady Mayor. That's not what I'm here to do,' he says, loud enough for me to hear. 'I'm here for a press conference.'

Twig fires a questioning look at me, as if he thinks I know what's going on. I shrug. And my blood starts to flow again.

While Dad's been speaking, Digby has pulled our old folding picnic table from the boot of his car. He sets it up so the banner hangs like a backdrop behind it. Then he rounds up the TV and radio crews and the journalists.

Meanwhile Dad has set his briefcase on the table and is taking out various documents and maps.

'OK,' Dad says to the waiting reporters, 'as you know, the town council has, in the last few days, approved plans for a new mega-mall multiplex to be built right here, on the site of Bluebell Wood.'

From the trees opposite someone starts up a chant again. 'HANDS OFF BLUEBELL WOOD! HANDS OFF BLUEBELL WOOD!'

Dad raises a hand for quiet. 'Bluebell Wood has been here since I was a boy,' he says. 'I played here. My daughters played here. It's too important a natural resource for us to destroy.'

The tree protestors cheer.

'But isn't it true, Mr Wilde,' one of the journalists asks, 'that most people in Strathcarron want the new development? That the town desperately needs better leisure facilities, and that it will bring much-needed jobs?'

'Yes. That's all true,' Dad says. 'And as someone who wants to represent the people of Strathcarron I want all those things too. But perhaps the Lady Mayor would like to tell us why she's chosen this particular site?'

The Lady Mayor looks coldly at Dad, then turns to the waiting journalists.

'Bluebell Wood was chosen after extensive feasibility studies. It's not just the best location, it's the ONLY available location –'

'So,' Dad interrupts her calmly, 'it has nothing to do with the fact that your husband is one of the developers, and the town council sold Bluebell Wood to his company at a knock-down price –'

'Exactly what are you saying?' the Lady Mayor snaps, her eyes ice cold.

'I'm saying that this whole deal is corrupt. And that you had no right to sell Bluebell Wood in the first place.' Dad lifts a bundle of yellowed papers tied with pink ribbon from the picnic table. 'Because these deeds state that Bluebell Wood is a protected site. It cannot be sold. Ever. To anyone!'

All manner of mayhem breaks loose then. The tree protestors cheer and whoop as the Lady Mayor spins on her heel and strides towards her car.

The journalists and TV cameras follow her, baying, 'Is this true, Lady Mayor?'

'Give us a statement!'

But she ignores them, slams her door and orders her chauffeur to drive off.

Up in the trees everyone's cheering, 'WE SAVED BLUEBELL WOOD! WE SAVED BLUEBELL WOOD!'

'We did it, Sassy!' Twig says, grinning. 'Well, with a little help from your dad!' Then he hugs me. And I'm so surprised I almost fall out of the tree. Again.

Everyone's delighted. Dad's still busy talking to the journalists, showing them the ancient documents, opening maps out on the table.

I don't wait around to hear what he's saying.

I just take my guitar and slope off quietly home. Twig comes with me to the end of my road. He seems kinda shy now.

'Can I see you again?' he asks, looking at me through his flop of hair. 'Soon?'

'Course you can.' I smile. 'I'll probably be grounded forever. But I guess you know where my window is.'

'So I can call any time?' He blushes pink, and for a split second I get that squidgy feeling inside. You know the one I usually only get when I see tiny panda cubs or baby seals?

'Any time.' I smile again.

'OK!' he grins, his face a deep pink now. 'See ya around!' And he disappears up the road.

Brewster bumbles towards me, sniffing the air, and I tickle his ears. Then I slip round to the back garden and climb up the tree. I don't want to see Mum. In fact I don't want to see anyone. Not for a while. I've got a lot to think about.

I climb in my window and close the curtains and lie down on the bed, exhausted. In a way, I'm happy. Because Bluebell Wood is safe. And I've kept my promise to Pip.

But I'm not totally happy. The election is tomorrow. The Bluebell Wood protest will be all over the news tonight and the voters are going to be fuming when they hear they're not getting their new shops, their new swimming pool, their skating rink, their cinema. They're hardly going to vote for Dad, the man who took their new shiny mega-mall multiplex away.

We might have saved the wood, I think as I pull my duvet over my head. *But there's no way Dad can win the election now. And it's all my fault.*

38

How wrong can you be?

I should have known Dad wasn't so stupid! The election was yesterday. And guess what? Dad won!

While I came home to weep all over my room and worry like a neurotic newt that I had ruined his political career forever, Dad was saving his own skin.

Remember all those papers Mum and Dad and Digby were so busy with? They were the same ones Dad showed to the reporters. The wrinklies had been taking the threat to Bluebell Wood seriously all along! They ploughed through all the old documents with a fine-tooth comb cos Dad suspected – rightly – that there might be a clause that would stop the sale of Bluebell Wood for development.

And remember Dad had gone to speak to the car-factory people? Well, after me and Twig left Bluebell Wood, Dad announced on nationwide

TV that he'd already found a new site for the mega-mall multiplex. It's going to be built on the car-factory site when it closes down – which otherwise would have become derelict and an eyesore. The people who work in the factory now will get new jobs building the new complex, and will be able to work in it afterwards.

So Dad worked out a solution where everyone – except the Lady Mayor – got what they wanted. And that, Digby says, won him the vote!

39

It's three days now since the election. Yesterday I had to go into school with Mum for a meeting with Mr Smollett about my exclusion.

'Sassy's father,' Mum explained to Mr Smollett, 'is unable to attend. He's too busy getting ready to take up his post as the newly elected Member of Parliament for Strathcarron.'

Smollett looked mightily impressed!

Of course, I had to sit through a long lecture about obeying authority blahblahblah, and then I had to agree never to lead any such wildcat protests again blahblahblah and to be a perfect pupil forever blahblahblah.

Then Smollett said I could go back to school, on condition I did some kind of service for the school community. So I'm starting up an Eco-awareness Group. We'll meet every Wednesday lunchtime and come up with ideas to make our school greener. Miss Cassidy and Miss Peabody, who were both given a professional misconduct warning for attending the protest, have offered to be supervising teachers, so it should all be cool. Mr Hemphead, apparently, is taking early retirement to spend more time with his stick insects, which was what he was wanting to do anyway.

40

It's Saturday evening. Cordelia and Taslima are here for a girls' night in. Taslima's really excited that Dad's an MP. She's got a new journal specially to note down observations of how my family copes with the stress of public office. She's even considering making a video diary of us.

There's an awful racket coming from Pip's room next door. She's practising a new dance routine: the Dance of the Endangered Dandelion. Pip's decided to be an eco-babe like me. I doubt it'll last. When Pip decided to go veggie she crumbled completely the first time she got a whiff of a bacon butty.

I bang on her wall to get her to turn it down a bit, then pick up my guitar and start tuning it.

'So what's happening about your demo disc?' Cordelia asks, fluttering her freshly painted purple fingernails in their lacy fingerless gloves.

'Not a lot,' I say, twanging a string. 'Dad says we had a deal. I broke it.'

'That's a bit hard,' says Cordelia. 'I mean, you did it for the right reasons.'

'But a deal is a deal,' Taslima interrupts in her professional psychiatrist's voice. 'Imagine the confusion it would cause if you made a promise, broke it, then got the reward anyway. It just wouldn't be right.'

'We've struck a new deal, though.' I twang another string. 'If I behave for the next three weeks, Dad says he'll reconsider his position.'

I twang the sixth string. 'Perfect. Right. Want to hear my latest song? It's not right yet, but it's kinda taking shape.'

'Cool.' Cordelia grins, tugging the latest copy of *Wiccan Weekly* from her skull-and-crossbones tote bag. 'Then I'll read out our horoscopes.'

'OK,' I say happily. 'It's called the Ballad of Bluebell Wood.'

> We were there in the trees
> There was Twig, there was me
> We were putting up a fight
> For what we knew was right.
>
> We wouldn't let them come
> With their axes and saws
> We protected the trees
> With our bodies, not laws.

Cos the world is a gift
Which we all need to share
With the oceans, the woods
And we all must take care.

We were there in the trees
There was Twig, there was me
We were putting up a fight
For what we knew was right.

By the time I get to the last line Taslima and
Cordelia are both helpless with laughter.

'"The Ballad of Twig", more like!' Taslima
sputters.

'At the protest,' Cordelia says, giggling so much
she can hardly speak, 'didn't I see you . . . share
a muffin . . . with Twig?'

'Wasn't a muffin,' I say innocently. 'It was a
doughnut. It meant nothing.'

'Yeah, but what about his fairy-thingies? You
might have got a whiff of them!' Cordelia insists,
fixing me with a don't-lie-to-me-or-I'll-turn-you-
into-a-mollusc stare.

'And what about that friendship bracelet?'
Taslima asks mischievously, eyeing the faded green
bracelet on my wrist. 'Who gave you that?'

'Well, Twig, obviously,' I reply, fingering it
gently. 'But just cos he's a boy and I'm a girl,
it doesn't mean –'

'Listen!' Cordelia interrupts, excitedly waving the *Wiccan Weekly*. 'You're Scorpio, right, Sass? Well, Psychic Psandra says: *Scorpio! Expect love in unexpected places* –'

Suddenly Taslima squeals and points at the window behind my head. Even before I turn I hear the sound of the whistle from the tree outside. Playing the tune for 'The Ballad of Bluebell Wood'.

'No! No! No!' I wail, leaping to my feet and tugging the curtains shut. As I throw myself down on my beanbag Taslima and Cordelia stare at me like I've just flipped.

'I've got the planet to save. And my singing career to get off the ground. I really don't have time to be in love!'

LAST TRACK

They give us plastic palm trees
They give us concrete walls
They make the waves with wave machines
They put up parasols.

They pull up all the trees and flowers
They poison all the seas
They make a waste of all that's ours
Roads spread like a disease.

They say this is de-vel-op-ment
Forget what they destroy
They fill our lives with grey cement
And then they say — ENJOY!

By Sassy Wilde

THANK YOU to . . .

Kiera and Hazel, my lovely daughters, for the
inspiration; Ian for his patience; Cathy for her
encouragement; my son, Stuart, for putting
up with me warbling on about Twig; Caroline
at David Higham Associates for her support;
Amanda for her amazing editorial input;
Sara for her fab cover design; Hennie for her
super-sassy artwork; and all the rest of the
Puffins, Sarah, Wendy, Louise, Tania and
Sophie, for being wonderful!

Join Sassy

on her next escapade

Coming in **August 2009**

...you'll love it!' – Cathy Cassidy

Maggi Gibson

Seriously Sassy

Pinch me, I'm dreaming

'I sing cos I care about things. I'm not gonna change just to be famous!'

She's a rock chick with eco attitude. For Sassy it's not all about fame.

But as Sassy's dreams start to come true, it's not just her guitar strings that are twanging – it's her heart-strings too . . .

Can Sassy stay true to her heart?

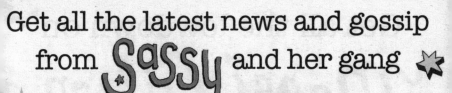

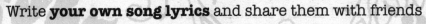

Get all the lowdown on

Maggi Gibson

Favourite book?
SCARLETT by Cathy Cassidy. It has everything I want in a book – great characters, funny bits, a terrific story – oh, and a dash of magic and romance.

Favourite song?
ONE LITTLE SONG by Gillian Welch. Not very well known, I know, but I love its simple lyrics and melody. Actually, I wish Sassy had written it.

Favourite film?
I love TEN THINGS I HATE ABOUT YOU. But I also adore LITTLE MISS SUNSHINE. It made me laugh so much I fell off the cinema seat and disgraced myself in front of my two daughters.

Favourite place in the world?
Balqhuidder (you say Bal-whid-der) in Scotland. I lived near there for a while. There are high mountains and two beautiful lochs. You have to go up a single track road to reach it and it all feels ancient and magical, like you might see fairies or ghosts at any minute. Cordelia would absolutely LOVE it!

Do you have a personal motto?
Only you can make your dreams come true!